Praise for the Peaks Saga...

"I remember fondly reading The Lion, The Witch, and The Wardrobe *when I was in middle school.* The Peaks at the Edge of the World *has a similar mix of fantasy and adventure with a moral tale at its center. This is a book that's appropriate for a younger audience than most sci fi/fantasy novels. Enjoy the read!"*

—Kathy Dunhoff
ZOLA AWARD-WINNING WOMEN'S FICTION WRITER

"...a page turner!" —Judith Seidel

"Ms. Erler puts religion in new settings as she uses the characters in both the past and the future to meld the consequences of a religion lost, then found, then challenged. The ride is exciting. The characters real and engaging."

—Charlene Hecht
BA MUSIC EDUCATION
LONGTIME WRITER, INCLUDING "GUNSMOKE" FAN FICTION

"M.F. Erler skillfully pioneers a new writing genre, mixing elements of science fiction, dimensional time-travel, and modern Christian spirituality. She uses likeable characters in well-crafted settings in which we can identify with their real-life struggles."

—Richard Bartlett, MA, PhD

"...[M.F.] Erler's book, with its futuristic sci-fi focus and true-to-life grittiness, is not your typical Christian novel. At times, it unabashedly describes the realities of the darkness of humanity in order to contrast it with the power of hope and love found in God's grace. This unique book is well worth your time to read and I highly recommend it."

—Pastor Kevin Bueltmann
TRINITY LUTHERAN CHURCH - ASSOCIATE PASTOR
TRINITY LUTHERAN CAMP - EXECUTIVE DIRECTOR

Books by M.F. Erler

THE PEAKS SAGA

PEAKS AT THE EDGE OF THE WORLD
Finding the Light

SEARCHING FOR MAIA

MOUNTAINTOPS AND VALLEYS

WHEN THE WORLD GROWS COLD

THE FOUNTAIN AND THE DESERT

BEYOND THE WORLD

WHERE ALL WORLDS END

MOUNTAINTOPS and VALLEYS

M.F. ERLER

MOUNTAINTOPS AND VALLEYS, Book 3
by M.F. Erler

Published by

WESTWIND PRESS
an imprint of First Steps Publishing
PO Box 571
Gleneden Beach, Oregon 97388-0571
FirstStepsPublishing.com

ISBN: 978-1-937333-70-6 (hb)
    978-1-937333-68-3 (pb)
    978-1-937333-69-0 (epub)

Bible quotes are from King James Version, and New International Version:
"Scripture taken from Holy Bible, New International Version (Registered Trademark) Copyright 1973,1978, 1984 by International Bible Society. Used by permission of Zondervan Publishing House. All rights reserved."

All lyrics quoted are Public Domain or composed by the author.

Cover illustration by Kabita Studios
Cover design, book formatting by Suzanne Fyhrie Parrott

Please provide feedback

10 9 8 7 6 5 4 3 2

Printed in U.S.A.

This Book is dedicated to Steve and Kaye,
friends and mentors from many years ago,
but each from a different time and life.

Contents

FOREWORD

MOUNTAINTOPS AND VALLEYS

I'm coming down now, not an easy process,
Not quite painful – yet
But that empty space is beginning to return
Deep inside me.

On the mountains are the highs:
A new friend – really discovering someone
A new idea – or the realization of an old one
Each new rush of excitement makes me want to take flight
And live forever in a world of such stimulation.

But now the ache is beginning
A tight spot in the chest,
Perhaps even a tear.
For I must go back to the valley now,
Back to the day-to-day challenges:
Of trying to be a whole person,
To accept life as it is, with its sameness—and emptiness.

Let me somehow take this 'high' from the mountain
And put it inside me –
To save it, incorporate it,
Treasure the memory, so I can use it
To find the high of even the small moments
And the low moments.

And still my tears start to fall,
I'm suddenly blinded.

I want to fly, not stay here on the ground…

So, I wonder: does anyone else feel this way?
Am I the only one?
Or do they just know how to adjust to the down-coming
Better than I?

And so I cling to this moment, this dream,
Knowing all the while
That it's gone – already –
Slipping through my fingers like water,
Shining and sparkling in the sunlight
Leaving empty hands, a lingering dampness,
Then that, too, is gone.

I'm left, like a dry bone, lying in the desert sun,
But even a dry bone has some secret life
—the minerals from which new life can come
In time:
After the decay, the soil,
Now the seed that sprouts,
Then the grazer—

So, I, too, must lie here and wait—
The things in me that once were alive
With hope and joy,
Will again be so – in their time.

Someday, somewhere, I will live again,
And perhaps in that life,
I'll live on the mountain,

Instead of always here in the Valley.

M. F. Erler

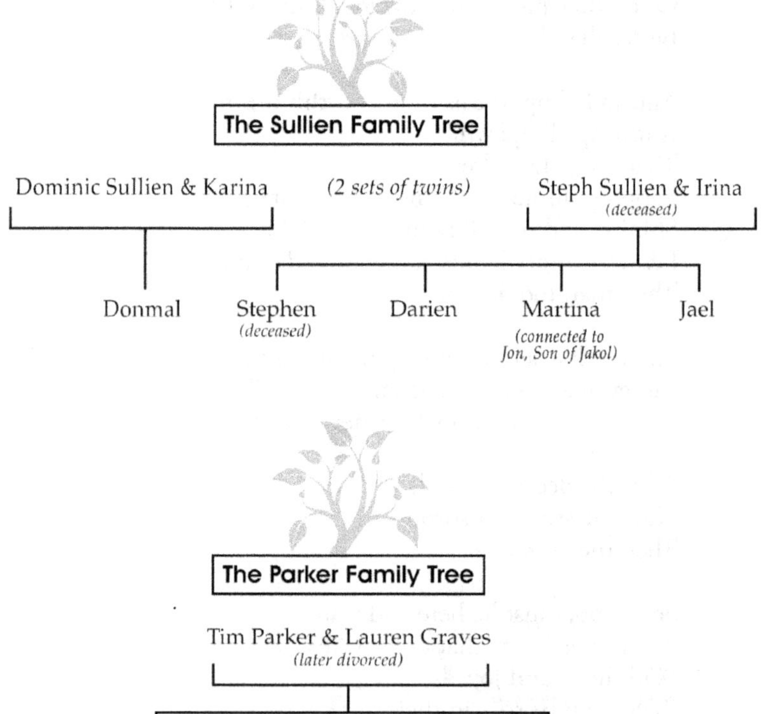
The Sullien Family Tree

Dominic Sullien & Karina
(2 sets of twins)
Steph Sullien & Irina
(deceased)

Donmal
Stephen
(deceased)
Darien
Martina
(connected to
Jon, Son of Jakol)
Jael

The Parker Family Tree

Tim Parker & Lauren Graves
(later divorced)

Ginna
(experimentally connected to Martina)
Danny
(experimentally connected to Jael)

CHAPTER 1

PRELUDE

"Well, I think it's about time for a female point-of-view in this tale."

"So do I, Ginna, but that's my job!" insisted Martina Sullien

"Come on, Martina, you know that I'm within you, and you are somehow part of me. And right now I'm talking to myself, or something—I guess."

"Well, remember we live in parallel worlds, but right now we're in my world, so that means you're me. Your turn will come if we go to visit your world."

"I still don't understand what this really means, Martina."

Jon, the eldest in the group, reached over and patted her shoulder. This in itself was strange because Martina and Ginna both felt his touch. "No one completely understands it—not even the quantum physicists who first postulated it. The more they explored the Universe, the more unexplained things they found."

"Like black holes?" asked Danny, Ginna Parker's younger brother.

Jon nodded. "And anti-matter."

"Dark matter, too," added Jael's voice.

"The Theory of Parallel Universes was one that came about as a result of these discoveries," said Jon. "Then, when the GAP was discovered, we found we could travel between some of them."

"But why do we sometimes have our own thoughts, even when we're 'within' someone else?"

"I'm not sure, Danny," Jon shrugged. "We're still exploring and learning about this."

"How come you get all the fun, Martina?" Ginna interrupted. "All I get to do is watch and listen. Am I supposed to learn something by being inside your mind?"

Jon looked at her with concern in his eyes.

"You know it's more than that," Martina replied. "You are 'within' me right now, so you get to really experience what I've been through. I hope it will help you in the long run."

"Okay, you're right. I _am_ feeling the same things that you do, maybe even more than I should. And I sort of feel at home 'inside' you now. When can we get on with your story, so I can keep living it?"

Jon frowned at this but said nothing.

"I thought you didn't like the idea of being 'inside' someone else," laughed Martina. "When Jon first proposed this Parallel Universe experiment, you were really hesitant. Remember?"

"Well, a girl can change her mind, can't she?"

"All right, we'll continue Martina's story soon," said Jon. "But first I need you to meet someone. We two aren't the only ones who need to tell our side of the story. To get this part told, we'll need to go back and forth through those 'blinds' a few times."

"You mean back and forth between our parallel worlds?"

"That's right, Ginna. So now, I need to take you and Danny back to your time and your own home to introduce you to someone."

***

Everything was dark around them suddenly. There weren't any stars in the sky. In fact, all they could see was snow swirling in the air around them.

Along with the cold wetness, Ginna felt a sudden desolation. She was just herself— alone again. In her heart, she knew Martina was gone, and it felt awful. 'I didn't know it would be like this,' she thought. 'I feel so empty without her. What do I do now?'

"Danny, where are you?" she screamed. She needed to *be* with someone right now. This aloneness was wrenching her heart, which felt like it was already broken into many pieces.

"Right here, Ginna! Reach out your hand!"

She reached with both hands and, on her left, she felt her brother's arm. She grabbed quickly and held on tightly.

"Hey, don't squeeze so hard!"

"Oops! Sorry, Danny. I just don't want to lose you."

"Are we back in Colorado?"

"I can't see anything with all this snow, but it sure feels like an eastern Colorado snowstorm."

Danny was groping with his free hand in the air, trying to find something—anything—solid. Then, he felt the rough wood. "Hey, Ginna, I think I've found the porch rail."

"Where?"

"Here." He led her to the only solid thing he could feel and put her hand under his.

"Yeah! I think it *is* our back porch."

Carefully, so as not to lose their grip, the two children groped their way along the railing. Then Ginna felt her foot hit something.

"Ouch! There's a step, I think. I just hit it."

She guided Danny to where her foot struck. "Yes," he said. "These are the back steps."

At last, they worked their way onto the porch, through the creaking back door, and tumbled into the house.

"Gosh! I never thought I'd be so glad to see our old kitchen," she said.

"Me neither."

"Why did they bring us back in a blizzard?"

"I don't think they meant to, Ginna. Sometimes the time factor can be off. Jael told me."

"Where are they anyway? I thought Jon said he wanted us to meet someone."

"I wonder if they got lost in the blizzard, too."

Just then there came a crashing sound on the porch,
and the back door flew open. Snow swirled into the kitch-
en, and along with it came Martina. Right behind her was
a smaller girl with red hair.

"Whew!" she cried. "I'm really sorry about the snow.
I'm new at this time-travel stuff."

"Martina!" Ginna grabbed her with a fierce grip.

"Watch it! Don't choke me, Ginna."

She released her grip, but still held onto Martina's
arm. "I feel so empty without you."

"Hey, it's okay," came another familiar voice.

Ginna felt Jon's arm across her shoulders. She found
herself leaning into him. "I feel like half my heart has been
torn away, Jon."

"You'll be okay," he rubbed the palm of her hand with
his thumb. This felt somehow familiar. It must be something he did with Martina often.

"I sure hope so," she sighed. She looked up at both
of them and realized with a start how strange it was to
see Martina with her own eyes, instead of seeing things
through Martina's eyes. 'Will I ever get to be inside her
mind again?' she thought wistfully.

"I'm sorry about the crossing," Jon was saying. "I was

putting too much stock in Ginna's being firstborn, and forgot how inexperienced she was."

Now Ginna looked at both of them in amazement. "You mean I have this GAP-crossing power, too?"

Jon nodded. "It would be better if you got some training in using it, though."

"I don't see how I can be here in the Twenty-first Century when it hasn't even been discovered yet," she sighed.

"That's true," he shrugged. "Anyway, when I realized there was a problem, I stepped into the GAP to help you." Jon took her hand. "I'm sorry."

For a moment, Martina looked angry, seeing Jon holding Ginna's hand, but she said, "Thanks, Honey." Then she turned to Danny and Ginna. "So, anyway, this is Raina."

"Hi, Raina," said Danny.

"She's Jason's sister from Terres."

"How did she escape the terrible fire and all?" Ginna asked.

"We're going to let her tell her whole story," Jon said.

Both of the children turned to Raina expectantly.

"You're welcome to sit on our old couch," said Ginna. "That seems to be where most of this GAP-crossing Time-Travel takes place."

Martina and Jon chuckled and followed Ginna into the tiny living room.

"When do I get to go back 'within' you, Martina?"

"Not for a while, Ginna. Raina needs to tell us her story. And I wasn't there for most of it."

Ginna let out a long sigh. "Okay, if we have to."

Jon was looking at her quizzically again, as though he was trying to decipher something in her face. Then he got out that strange fluted lamp they'd seen before.

"So, here we are again," he said. "Are you ready, Raina?"

"Yes, Jon."

The swirling colors from the lamp danced around the walls of the room. Ginna focused her eyes on Raina, though. 'She looks close to my age,' she thought. 'I hope her story can help me feel better about living in this place and time, a place that doesn't feel like home to me now.'

Raina's voice began with a sort of wordless chant, a different sound than they'd heard before. When she started to weave her story, the colors from the lamp became redder than ever before. Soon they found themselves in the middle of a raging inferno.

CHAPTER 2

RAINA'S STORY

The heat was awful, and I knew I couldn't take much more of it. I kept trying to run away from the flames, but they were always close behind me. The loud crackling sounds were almost as bad as the heat. It was as though some hungry monster was trying to catch me.

'Where's Jael?' my anguished mind kept asking. All I wanted to do was find him.

I had no idea where my older brother Jason was. He'd left our house early that morning and not returned. Mother and Father were gone to their respective jobs. Now they should be coming home. I'd watched the sun setting in the east, as it always did on our planet Terres.

But today was anything but ordinary. Suddenly, or so it seemed, another sun came too close to our sun, Regelian. (The result had been our entire solar system being dragged through space, though I really didn't understand that at the time.) What I did know was that a swirl of hot gases and flames crossed our planet's path, and now it seemed all of Terres-City was ablaze.

'Why didn't Jael take me with him?' I kept asking in my mind. We'd been close friends for a long while now. But recently, he seemed to draw away from me, and I couldn't understand why. Now this disaster had come, and I didn't know how to find him, though he mattered much more to me than my family did.

We'd met at Anha's house before we were quite old enough for school. His father died in the wars, he told me, and his mother was taken to the Institute. All that remained were his two brothers and one sister, all much older than he was. I was only there at Anha's because both my parents worked away from home in the center-city, but he had no one else to care for him.

While he was there at Anha's, his oldest brother, Stephen, died in a shuttle crash. Then his brother, Darien, went away to join the Inland Raiders. And, as though this weren't enough, his sister ran away to the Wilds to join the Redlarks. He was totally alone in the world. That was when he came to live at our house.

I tried to do all I could to befriend him. For a long time, he didn't seem able to get out of the shell of grief he was in. Finally, my gift to him of a feier-cat helped him come back to the everyday world. But we weren't attending the same school there in Terres-City, because he kept going to the one designated for his home neighborhood.

That was probably why we hadn't seen as much of each other recently, even though he'd been staying at my house for several months now. In my home, people kept to themselves mostly.

We were both about ten Standard Years old when he came. This past month, I had my eleventh nameday, and Jael gave me a book he liked to read. I didn't have the heart to tell him that I still couldn't read words on paper. I'd been taught in the new Councilar School where we did everything on a Terminal, where old-style reading and writing weren't necessary.

Still, I cared a lot for Jael, even though he was distancing himself from me. He seemed to think my brother Jason had something to do with the so-called vandals who trashed his house and burned all their antique books. I had no idea who did it, but I didn't like to think my brother had anything to do with it.

Jason was dating Jael's sister, Martina, and taking her to the Underground with him before she ran away. Jael and I were too young for the Underground, but we knew what it was, a place where people could let all their inhibitions go, where no one would judge anyone for their actions, and people could do as they pleased. But then Martina and Jason fought, and she ran away. Jael was sure she'd gone to the Redlarks.

So now here I was, fleeing the fire that was consuming the city, my home for all my short life. I wasn't at all sure that I'd have this life much longer. Then, up ahead I saw a blank spot in the blazing inferno. There appeared to be a pool of some kind.

Yes! It was the pool surrounding a fountain on the eastern edge of the city's central park. Without even thinking about it, I plunged into the water. It was getting warm from being so close to the flames, but it was wet. I dove under to get my head wet, too. Then, hopefully, my hair wouldn't catch fire.

As I sat there dripping and thinking how wonderful it felt, I saw a woman sitting close beside me. Her eyes were glazed over, and her wet dark hair was plastered to her head.

"Hello?" I said, moving closer so my elbow touched hers.

"Hello," she whispered hoarsely. "What's your name?"

"I'm Raina. Who are you?"

"My name is Irina. What are we going to do?"

I shrugged. It was a good question, but I had no answers. "I'm trying to find a friend," I said.

"I wish I could find my children." But she didn't say more, because then she broke into great sobs and put her head in her hands. I tried to give her a hug, but she made no response.

"Do you know where they are?" I asked, feeling I needed to do something to help her, though I had no idea what.

"No!" she sobbed all the louder. "The Council took me from them. I don't know what happened to them, and they don't know what's become of me, either."

"How long ago was this?"

"I really have no idea," she murmured. "The drugs have taken all time-sense from me."

I couldn't think of anything else to say, and she seemed to have lost her train of thought.

At this moment there came cries and shouts:

"Look out!"

"Neptune Spire!"

"It's going to fall!"

We jumped up as if by reflex and began to run toward the edge of the park. Irina kept stumbling, but I managed to pull her up and keep her going with me. Behind us, there were awful crashing and groaning sounds, and cries of pain and dismay. I just kept on pulling her along with me, and somehow we got out of there.

I don't remember much else after that. I must have been in a daze as I moved along. My body just kept on trying to save itself, even after my mind shut down.

****

The next thing I knew, I was lying on my back, with dark clouds floating in the sky above me. I gingerly felt all my limbs and found nothing was broken. There were a few scorched places on my clothes, but my hair was still on my head. I have red hair and freckles, which I don't like. But I remembered then Jael was always fascinated by them, and the thought of him brought the ache back to my heart.

As I was thinking, I heard a sigh and the sound of someone coughing nearby. Looking over, I saw Irina, the woman I'd found in the fountain pool. Her eyes were glazed over again, and she made no response when I called her name. Still, she let me pull her to her feet.

"Come on," I said. "We need to move farther away from the City."

I wasn't sure why I said this, but I just didn't want to stay near that smoldering, ruined place any longer.

She still didn't say anything but walked along beside me in a mechanical sort of way. We kept this slow walking pace up for most of the daylight period. I had no idea what time it was, or even if time could be measured as it was before. With our sun captured by its new twin star and dragged to a new location in the Galaxy, who had any idea how long our days and years would be now?

So Irina and I just walked and stumbled our way away from Terres-City and into the Wilds. There were no other cities on Terres for us to flee to. The only other place where there might be inhabitants was the camps of the Redlarks. My brother Jason had told me a little about these runaways from city life.

"They're no better than barbarians," he said. "They seem to think they're free out there, away from the Council and the System. But they've given up all the good things living here in the City can offer."

This attitude about the Redlarks probably explained why he was so upset when Martina ran away to join them. He had no intention of going after her, he said, "To me, she's already non-existent."

Days and nights flowed along for what seemed forever, as Irina and I kept on walking toward the east. This was the direction Jason seemed to indicate whenever he spoke of the Redlarks. Sometimes we'd see figures in the distance, but they were always too far away to hear my calls.

After the first night, I was famished. Sometime the next day, I managed to find some berries for us and begged Irina to eat something, but all she did was gaze into space and walk when I pulled her along. Otherwise, she seemed frozen into a blank stare.

I don't think we could have gone much farther when I finally saw some figures who were near enough to be in earshot.

"Help!" I heard myself calling. "Please help us."

One of them turned toward us. I could see it was a young man with dark hair, so I knew it wasn't my brother, for Jason had red hair like mine. I waved both arms over my head, to get them to see us better, and began pulling Irina in their direction. At this point, I didn't care who or what they were. They were the only other humans we'd seen for several days.

"Halloo!" one of them called. "Are you from the City?"

"Yes!" I shouted back.

Soon, we were close enough for me to see that there were three of them. The tallest was a willowy young woman, whose clothes were nearly in rags. The young man with the dark hair was holding her hand. Behind them was another man, with a gray beard, who hobbled as though his feet hurt. I'd never seen any of them before.

"What are your names?" the young man asked. "I'm Amian."

"My name is Raina. And this is Irina."

"Your mother?" asked Amian.

"No. I just found her in the park and brought her with me. We have no idea where any of our families are."

"Well, I also found Myra and brought her," he said. "The old man is Jakob, her father."

"Did you lose your family, too?" I asked.

"Not in the disaster, no," he said. "They were lost to me long ago, when I first went to the Redlarks."

"Do you know how to find the Redlarks?" I asked, my hope rising slightly.

"Yes. We're heading in the direction of a camp I know."

"May we please come with you? I have nowhere else to go."

"What about Irina?"

"Her either, I guess. She's stopped speaking, and hasn't said a word since we left the City."

"Well then, we might as well travel together. There's more safety in numbers," said Amian.

And so we set out, the five of us. Amian seemed to know his way fairly well. Finally, I asked him how long he'd been with the Redlarks.

"It's several Standard Years now," he replied. "I'm usually sent back and forth to the City—to recruit new members, you know." He winked at me as he said this.

"Do the Redlarks actually try to get people to come join them?"

"Oh yes! Why not? We need new talents and new gene pools."

"I guess that makes sense," I shrugged. I was hoping that Amian realized I was still too young to add to his gene pool. There was something about the way his sparkling eyes looked at me that made me feel uncomfortable.

Fortunately, it was only a couple of days' travel until we saw the first of the camps. Nestled in a green valley, with snowcapped peaks beyond, was a cluster of huts. They blended so well with the landscape that they were hard to distinguish until we got much closer to them.

A couple of people who were gathering berries spotted us first.

"Amian!" called one. "What have you brought us this time?"

"Halloo!" he replied. "This may be the last trip."

"What?"

Soon, several other people were gathering around us, and many questions were being fired at Amian. He waved a hand and walked straight toward the largest hut in the camp. Once we reached it, he stopped us all and gave a strange bird-like whistle.

The doorway of the hut was soon shadowed by a figure wearing a feather headdress. He looked carefully at each of us and then motioned for the five of us to follow him into his hut.

Once we were settled, he drew out a stick covered with tally marks of some kind and made four more marks on it.

"That will be the last, I'm afraid," said Amian.

"Yes, we've been told the City has burned with the coming of the Sign," said this man I took to be a chief. "So who's come with you this time, my dear agent?"

"This girl-child is Raina, and with her is Irina, who is not her mother." He nodded at me. "They found each other in the flight from the disaster, same as I also found Myra and her father, Jakob."

"What is your wish now, Amian?" he asked.

"I would request a hut for Myra and her father, and another one for Raina and Irina."

"And for yourself—for all your years of service to us?"

Amian looked down for a moment, and then at me. "I would like Raina for myself," he said.

The chief looked from him to me and then nodded his head. I felt a cold lump in the pit of my stomach. Was I just being treated like property?

But there was no one to speak up for me. Irina was staring, as she had for days on end. Myra and Jakob were still practically strangers to me. I had no one to defend me.

"Sir?" I finally managed to gasp. "Have I no say in this? I'm still a child."

The chief looked carefully at me and chuckled. "Yes, so you are. Amian, I think you must wait awhile to claim your woman—until she becomes a woman."

"Very well, my chief." Amian bowed low to the ground. "May I help her build her hut?"

"Yes," said the chief, and then we were dismissed.

***

So, over the next several days, a small hut was built for Irina and me. Meanwhile, I was taught how to gather the edible fruits and vegetables, by one of the women of a nearby hut. Irina learned to weave strips of soft brown bark, along with stringy grasses, into a roof for our hut and clothes for us to wear. But she still seemed to have forgotten how to speak.

One day, much too soon for my taste, Amian came and asked if he might come in.

"I suppose," I said. But I made sure Irina was close by.

"What do you want of me, Amian?" I asked as if I didn't know.

"Will you consent to be my woman?" He came right out with it.

"Do I have any choice?"

"Well, I'm trying to give you one." He smiled, but his eyes still had a glint which made me nervous.

"Then my answer today is, no," I whispered.

"What about tomorrow, or another day?"

"Perhaps. I'm too young now. Please give me time."

"Very well. I need to make a journey to the camps beyond the river. That will take a few months. Perhaps by then, you'll be ready."

I only nodded. It didn't seem right of me to wish him ill, but in the back of my mind, I was hoping he wouldn't get back from this trip of his.

CHAPTER 3

THE CRIME

Just before he left on his journey, Amian forced himself on me. I was gathering berries to make fruit-leather, one of the main things The People used to sustain themselves on their travels. Ironically, it was actually for him.

I was far enough from the camp that no one could hear my cries for help, as he pulled me into a thicket not far from the river. Once he stripped me and begun placing his hands in all my private places, I lost my voice. I guess I was trying to wall my inner self into a closed place, where he couldn't reach me. Perhaps he'd have my body, but he wouldn't have my true self—ever.

He never said a word once he started. His hands and body did too much talking, anyway. The pain for me was awful, partly because I was still small for my age. I was only eleven.

Once he satisfied himself, he rose, pulled up his trousers, and walked away without a word. I must have lain there for a long time, too numb to move a muscle. Finally, I managed to pull my clothes back on and tried to stand. The world whirled around me, and I sank back to the ground into a small huddle of misery. All I wanted to do at that moment was die. This is where Irina found me.

She didn't say anything—she still hadn't spoken a word since we'd left the City. But I could tell she knew what had happened. Gently, she gathered me into her arms and carried me back to our hut. Once there, she didn't set me down, but sat close to our tiny cooking fire and rocked me, as both of us shed many tears.

I must have fallen asleep, for when I woke it was night. Still, Irina was holding and rocking me. At last, I found my voice, and said the only name I could think of at that moment, "Jason." Somehow, I thought, if my older brother were here, this wouldn't have happened. But Jason wasn't here, and I had no idea if I'd ever see him again. The next name I spoke was, "Jael."

Irina stirred suddenly when she heard me speak this name. "Jael," she whispered. "My dear little boy."

But then she lapsed back into her silence and seemed to go back to sleep.

So did I. The next time I awoke, the first rays of dawn were peeking in through our hut's doorway.

This time, Irina was awake, and I could see her looking at me intently. I wanted so much to hear her voice that I looked straight into her eyes and asked, "Who is Jael?"

She looked very surprised at my question. "He's my youngest child."

"And how many children do you have?"

"Four. I have four children, and only one is a girl like you. I can't help them now. Please let me help you."

I leaned on her shoulder then. "Yes, please help me." Then I began to sob. I hadn't meant to cry, but the tears just came gushing from my eyes. "Please help me get away from him."

"Who did this to you?"

"Amian."

I heard her groan deeply at this. "He's left on his journey now."

"But he'll come back for me, I'm sure."

"Yes, we must find a way to escape before he does come back," she said.

This was the most I'd ever heard her say. Perhaps having the chance to be a mother again was reviving her. I wasn't sure if I should bring up the name Jael again, but I did anyway.

"I knew a boy named Jael," I whispered. "He was about my age, and he was my best friend. We met at Anha's."

"Yes, Anha." She seemed to be trying to bring out very old memories. "She was my neighbor."

"I met his sister Martina, too," I added.

"That's my daughter's name." Now there was a great surprise in her voice.

"She was older than Jael."

"Yes! Why were they at Anha's?"

"Their mother had been taken to the Institute."

"I was! Yes, they took me away, and I never saw my children again."

Now I could hear the heartbreak in her voice. She must be Jael and Martina's mother! I didn't think she was ready to handle the news of Stephen's death, though, so I didn't mention it. Instead, I snuggled into her arms again.

"My mother is gone," I said. "I don't know where any of my family ended up in the disaster. And I really need someone now."

As if by instinct, she began to rock me again. "I'll take care of you," she whispered.

We stayed in the hut the rest of that day. She boiled some water on the cooking fire and helped me clean myself up. As I washed, I wondered if I'd ever feel whole again. It was as if Amian had taken part of me that I could never replace. I looked up at Irina and said, "Was it my fault? What should I have done?"

"It's *not* your fault!" she said quickly. "Please never think that. It was in his eyes from the start. I saw it, but I was the one who did nothing to protect you."

Tears were coming to her eyes now.

"No, Irina! Please, you mustn't blame yourself, either."

"But what can I do now?" she continued.

"You can take care of me," I said, taking her hand. "We have to find a way to escape."

"Yes, we must."

***

The next day, snow was falling from the sky, so we put on all our clothing to keep out the cold and ventured out of our hut. I knew Myra and Jakob's hut was nearby, so I took Irina there.

Myra answered my knock and motioned for us to come inside. She looked much better since she was rid of her ragged clothes. Jakob also seemed stronger now that he was able to eat and sleep in more normal circumstances.

"Are you doing well?" I asked, trying to be friendly.

"Yes, are you?" she replied.

"I could be better." I tried to begin my story myself, but my voice broke and betrayed me right away.

Irina took my hand and said, "Amian raped her."

There—my shame was out in the open for all to see. Suddenly tears were in Myra's eyes, and Jakob jumped up and grabbed his large walking stick, holding it more like a club. "That beast!" he roared.

"He's gone on a journey," Irina said then. "We must find a way to escape before he gets back."

Jakob sat down again and motioned for all of us to join him in their fire circle. He didn't speak for a long time but sat deep in thought. At last, he whispered, "I may be able to contact friends who can help us."

"How can we find them?" Myra asked.

"What kind of friends?" asked Irina.

Jakob didn't answer either of them but took my hand.

I almost pulled it back by reflex, before I managed to tell my mind that not all men were evil. "It's a dangerous thing to try to make contact like this, but I will do it for our dear girl-child."

I was amazed to hear these words from him, for I hadn't really talked with him much on our journey from the city. I thought he hardly knew me.

"She's all alone in the world," Irina said. "We're her only friends and have been entrusted with her care by the True Lord of the Universe. We must do what we can for her."

These words didn't make any sense to me. Who in the world was this True Lord? How could he have anything to do with what happened to me in the past few weeks? Still, I was thankful for the result, for Myra took my other hand as she joined hands with Irina.

Now we were all joined in a circle of hands, and I saw the three of them close their eyes as Jakob spoke softly, "Oh Lord, our God. Give us strength and wisdom as we seek how we can help this child, Raina."

Then they all sat in silence for a few moments. No one opened their eyes, but I kept gazing from one of them to the other. Their faces seemed to have become more peaceful, and less hopeless. I felt Myra squeeze one of my hands, and Jakob did the other.

When they opened their eyes, Myra smiled at me. "We'll find a way. Please don't let this drive you to despair."

"I know what despair can do," Irina said. "For I let myself be consumed by it when my husband, Steph, died. And the result was I lost my children, too."

"Your husband was named Stephen?" I found myself asking.

"No, that was my eldest son. Did you meet him?"

Now I was in trouble, for I had to answer, and it didn't seem right to lie to these people. "No, he died in a shuttle crash shortly after I met Jael and Martina. I'm so sorry, Irina."

She sat in shocked silence then, and I was afraid she'd go back into her catatonic state.

But then Myra took her hand and whispered, "Both of them are with the Lord now. I know your grief is great, but there's no need for despair."

I saw Irina nod. Then she turned back to me, "What about Darien?"

"He joined the Inland Raiders."

She seemed to feel better at this. "Well, at least he didn't perish in the disaster of Terres-City."

"Maybe Martina didn't either," I said. "She ran away to the Redlarks before the disaster. And Jael may be with Jon."

"Jon?"

"My brother Jason's friend. He was a Redlark, too."

"Then perhaps they're somewhere in the camps beyond the river," said Myra.

"That's where Amian was going," I whispered.

"Then we shouldn't go there now," said Jakob. His voice began to take on a tone of command like he was used to making decisions.

"If we could find my brother-in-law Dominic…" Irina began.

"Dominic?" Myra and Jakob said together. "The Twin?"

"Yes, he's my husband's twin brother."

"He's been one of our chief contacts here in the Wilds," said Myra.

We all stared at each other for a few minutes. How could it be possible we had so many links that none of us knew of before? Had we come together by mere chance?

"This is a miracle," Myra whispered.

"God works in strange ways," Jakob added. "Myra, we must try to contact Dominic. Perhaps he can find a way for us to get off-planet."

Myra nodded and began putting on heavy clothes. I knew she was going to venture into the snow.

"Off-planet?" I said. "You mean we can actually leave Terres?"

"Yes, child," Jakob nodded, and I almost saw him smile. "We'll find a way to keep you safe from that beast Amian."

I smiled back at him. It was the first time I'd felt anything close to hope in a long while.

CHAPTER 4

THE SIGNAL TREE

When Myra returned, her clothes were covered with sticky wet snow. She took off her outer wrap close to the hut's door, so less snow got on the floor or near the cooking fire. She looked very cold and tired, so none of us asked her any questions until she was settled and warming her hands by the fire.

"There's been a fire in parts of the forest," she said at last.

"It must have been started by the disaster, or spread from the City," Jakob nodded.

"It was difficult for me to find the Signal Tree," Myra continued. "Many of the trees around it were scorched."

I wanted to ask what this Signal Tree was but decided they'd tell me if I needed to know.

"Were you able to leave any message?" asked Jakob.

"I had to be make-shift about it. And I have no idea how long it will be before anyone finds it. With so many people fleeing the city, refugees are flooding the camps."

"Yes, we've seen them here, too," said Jakob.

'Refugees like us,' I said to myself. 'Is there any chance Jael could turn up here?' I clung to this hopeful thought.

The others continued their discussion while I was thinking, and I missed part of what Jakob was saying:

"—sometime in the next month." I heard this, and then he stopped.

Irina took my hand and sighed. "I guess we'll be safe enough. Amian won't be back for at least that long."

"All we can do now is wait," Myra said.

I didn't like to think of doing nothing but waiting, but there was no other choice.

Irina rose to her feet then and took me with her. Slowly we put on our warm clothes again and stepped out into the cold outdoors.

Snow was still falling, and the impressions our shoes made when we came were full of snow. You could barely see the path we'd taken. Irina seemed to remember the way, though, so I kept hold of her hand. The trees looked strange with their branches bent down by the weight of the snow. Some of them were almost doubled over. The world seemed to have changed from browns and greens to black and white.

When we got back to our hut, it was very cold inside. Soon, however, Irina started a fire, and we sat as close to it as we dared, trying to keep warm. Eventually, she drew me into her lap, and our body-heat helped each of us keep the other warmer.

***

And so we waited. The snow fell for several days, only stopping occasionally for our new double sun to peek out from the clouds. Then the now-naked trees threw stark shadows on the white and frozen ground. I wondered if all our planet was covered with snow. Occasionally, Jakob or Myra would come by to see how we were doing, but there was never any news about Dominic.

Irina and I tried to forget our worries, especially the fear of when Amian would come back. She prepared small meals for us, and I did the best I could to find roots or dried fruits beneath the white blanket covering the forest. Myra and Jakob often brought us what they could spare. "We're becoming very indebted to them," Irina said.

I got a piece of wood and used one of our food knives to make a notch each time the sun set. It seemed the nights were much longer during this cold time. I wasn't sure if it was because of where we were in latitude, or because of the changes brought by our new sun.

One evening as I counted, there were over sixty notches on my stick. I'd soon be out of room to add any more and still, there was no word about Dominic.

Finally, though, the days seemed to last a little longer,

and the sunlight that came periodically felt warmer. Each day, the piles of white, and now dirty gray seemed to shrink. At last, one morning I woke to the sound of birds.

"Irina," I exclaimed. "Has winter finally ended?"

She smiled at me and nodded, one of the few times I'd seen her do this. "Yes, Raina, I do believe the winter has finally let go of the world."

Now when I ventured out, I'd have to be careful of puddles of water and muddy patches of ground. But I didn't mind because it meant the land was reawakening. I would get down low to the ground where I could see the tiny green plants pushing their way out of the soil.

After several more notches on my stick, I began to find flowers of yellow, white, and purple beginning to show their heads.

It was on one of these explorations of the woods around our camp that I found what I thought might be their Signal Tree. It was a towering evergreen, so tall that the branches with needles were high above me, almost out of sight. When I stretched my arms at full length, trying to encircle the tree, my hands didn't even meet.

As I looked up the trunk, I suddenly saw a strange shape formed in some of the tree's flaky bark. It seemed to be a diagram or cipher of some kind almost invisible in the contours of the bark. But I knew it was man-made, not natural, because of its color. 'Perhaps this is the message Myra left,' I thought excitedly.

Then I saw another cipher nearby, on the opposite side of the tree. Was this our long-awaited reply? I was so excited that I ran and skipped all the way back to our hut.

I took Irina back with me to look at the tree, but she didn't know what the ciphers might mean. So, once again, all we could do was wait, because Myra and Jakob weren't to be found anywhere in camp that day.

At last, one bright sunny morning, both Myra and Jakob came to our hut. I was excited because I felt sure this meant they had good news.

But Jakob's eyes looked troubled when he got close enough for me to see them. "We must talk inside," he said to us, as we all ducked into our hut.

"What is it? What's wrong?" asked Irina.

"We have a message from the Signal Tree," said Myra, "But..."

"Dominic cannot come to us. We must go to him." Jakob finished for her.

"Will it be far?" I asked.

"Perhaps. We don't know yet. I'm sorry," Jakob continued. "I'd hoped for something less difficult for our girl-child, and for my old knees." He chuckled a bit, and I thought, 'He's just trying to make me feel better.'

"We must start preparing right away," said Irina. "Amian could be back soon, with the weather breaking."

Myra nodded. "We have packs of food prepared. You and Raina just need to pack your clothing and any other necessities. But remember whatever you bring you must carry in your pack-sack."

***

We left with first light the next morning. Jakob led us north out of the camp, toward a high ridge that blocked the view beyond. As we picked our way over rocks and roots approaching this ridge, he pointed out the Redlark watchers at their posts.

"As soon as we are out of their sight, we'll reverse our direction," he said.

I wanted to ask him where he'd learned all these strategies, but he didn't seem very talkative that day.

Myra and Irina took turns walking close beside me. I guess they felt they would protect me better this way. I just tried to keep pace with the adults. They had longer legs than mine, and my pack-sack seemed to be gaining weight as the day wore on.

We finally turned back south by the middle of the afternoon. Soon the sun was sinking toward the eastern horizon. Jakob seemed to be looking for a particular place to make camp. Finally, he nodded and pointed to a cave halfway up a steep bluff.

"How will we ever get all the way up there?" asked Irina. I was thinking the same thing.

"We know a path," said Myra. So, she was experienced with this sort of thing, too. 'Who are these people?'

I wondered to myself. 'They certainly aren't like any city-dwellers I knew.'

While I was thinking this, I glanced over at Irina, but she was smiling to herself and didn't seem worried. This made me feel better.

Jakob led us up a narrow trail, and suddenly there were hand-carved steps in the rock above us. These were much easier going than the rough path we'd been on. As I climbed I wondered where these steps came from and decided this night I would get some answers.

Once we reached the cave, Jakob held up a hand to stop us before we went in. He motioned silently that he would check inside first. We waited, almost holding our breaths, as Jakob went in alone. Soon, however, he stuck his head out the opening and smiled. "All clear."

Then we crawled in. The adults couldn't stand because of the low ceiling of the cave, but I could in most places. I bumped my head once on a low spot, though, so I learned to be more careful.

The first thing they all did was to sit in a circle and join hands, while Jakob talked to their unseen Lord again. He seemed to be thanking him for helping us find our way. I had many questions but wasn't sure yet how to ask them.

Jakob decided it was too risky to light a cooking fire. "People could see the light for kilometers," he said. "We must get closer to the Far Wilds first."

While Myra and Jakob were getting food out that we

didn't have to cook, Irina and I laid out bedrolls. "Irina?" I whispered.

"Yes?"

"What are Jakob and Myra? They aren't Redlarks, but they seem to know the Wilds. They can't be city-dwellers like us."

"They know Dominic," she answered. "That tells me they are Rebels. And Believers."

"What are Believers?"

"People who remain loyal to the True King, the Lord of the Universe. There are very few of us left."

I heard the 'us', which answered one of my questions, at least. "So, you are one of these Believers?"

"Yes, Raina, I am."

"Your children, Martina and Jael, were they Believers, too?"

"I taught them what I could," she sighed. "They were still young when I…" Her voice broke, and I thought she was going to stop, but she went on, "I failed them when I let myself be consumed by grief for my husband. And now I've lost them all. But the Lord is still good—he brought you and me together."

"But, Irina, I don't understand who this Lord is. Where does he live? Will we ever see him? How can you talk to someone who isn't even here?"

"He reigns from Maia. But he's also spirit and can be many places at once."

I'd never heard of anything like this. So, I decided to ask another question, "Jael said your family kept ancient books and learned to read them. Why?"

"We believed it was better to read the words as they were originally written, so we could see for ourselves what they said."

"But you can hear the words on a Terminal."

"Yes, but how could we know whether the Council changed those words to suit themselves?"

"Couldn't they change the book, too?"

"Oh, they tried to, but if someone could find an older one, it would still have the truth there in print. It is much more difficult to change books because every single copy must be changed—or burned."

"And that's why they burn books when they can."

"Yes."

"Jael came to live at my house after all his books were burned."

"All of them?" There was great sadness in her voice.

"I'm afraid so."

"Oh, Steph and I worked so hard to have all those books for our family." Tears began to slip down her cheeks.

I took her hand. "It's all right. Jael told me he read all of them, and could remember most of them."

"So that's what the Lord planned for him." she murmured, almost to herself.

"What?"

"Jael had special talents. He could read and remember everything at a very young age. We wondered what special plans the Lord had for him. But now, perhaps he's…"

"I'm sure Jael escaped, Irina! He was always looking for Jon, and Jon would head back to the Redlarks as soon as the Sign came. I can feel somehow inside myself that Jael is not dead." I squeezed her hand.

"What is this Sign?" she asked.

"Jael said Jon talked of it all the time. I think it is what we call the disaster, the coming of the double-star."

Just then, Jakob crept up close to us. I'd noticed him examining the back wall of the cave very carefully, and wondered if he'd found another cipher there about how to find Dominic. But he didn't say anything as we sat down to eat some of the fruit-leather Myra handed us.

By the time we finished eating our evening meal, it was full dark outside and inside the cave. We crawled into our bedrolls and quickly fell asleep, tired from the long day's walk.

***

Just as light was reaching its way into the cave, I felt someone nudge me awake. Opening my eyes, I saw Jakob with his finger to his lips, telling me to keep silent. He motioned with his head toward the cave entrance, and I crept over there with him. Then he pointed toward the valley road below us, which we had crossed yesterday.

As my eyes adjusted to the sunlight, I finally made out two figures walking on the road. They seemed to be talking together, both with pack-sacks on their backs. Their clothes were rumpled and dirty like they'd traveled a long way.

After I watched for a few seconds more, I realized with a shock I knew who they were. One was short and dark, and certainly looked like Amian. The other figure was tall and slim with wavy blond hair. 'That could be Jon,' I thought. 'But what's he doing with Amian? And why isn't Jael with him?'

I pulled myself back into the cave and looked up at Jakob.

"So it *is* the beast?" he asked.

I nodded. Just seeing him, even at a distance, caused a tight ball of fear to form in my stomach.

"And the other?"

"I'm not sure," I heard myself say. I didn't want to think perhaps it *was* Jon. In fact, I didn't want it to be him! I wanted him to be somewhere safe with Jael, and I certainly did *not* want him to be friends with my rapist.

"Well, it's fortunate we left yesterday and not today," Jakob whispered. "The Lord is good."

Suddenly, for reasons I couldn't understand, I was furious. Balling my hands into fists, I began to pound on Jacob's chest. "How can your Lord be good? He let the beast violate me!" I sobbed.

Jakob didn't try to stop me, but let me keep on pounding on him until I collapsed into a heap. Then he gathered me into his arms as I continued to sob, and began to hum some unfamiliar tune. It did have a soothing sound, and I felt my anger gradually melt away.

"Dear, sweet little girl," he said. "We're mere mortals and can't know what the Lord has in store. But we do know he loves us, and whatever happens, he'll see us through. I'm sure he weeps with you for the crime done to you. It wasn't his plan that this happened, but somehow he'll bring good out of this terrible thing, someday."

"I don't know this Lord of yours," I muttered, clinging to him now. "I'm afraid of what will happen to me next."

"It appears he wants us to help you, Raina. Do you see how he has helped us leave the Redlarks' camp just in time?"

I nodded mutely.

"Well, that shows he hasn't abandoned us. We must keep on trusting and doing our best."

By this time, Myra and Irina were also awake. Jakob told them about seeing Amian on the road, but I didn't say anything about his companion. We quickly ate our breakfast and packed up. Soon we were picking our way down the cliff again. But Jakob turned us off onto a narrow side trail instead of taking us back to the valley road.

CHAPTER 5

HE RETURNS

We'd been trekking for many days when we came to what Jakob called the Great River. He seemed to know exactly where we were now.

"I wish we had a boat," he said. "It would be much easier."

But we didn't, so we had to work our way along the banks of the river, battling thick underbrush for many kilometers before we found a safe place to cross. Even then, I felt I was about to be swept away by the water at any moment. When we finally slogged out on the opposite bank, I was drenched, and my teeth were chattering with cold.

When Jakob saw this, he gathered me into his arms and actually carried me for awhile. I didn't think a man so old could be so strong. Being out here in the Wilds seemed to have brought him new vigor.

That night, he insisted that we start a campfire, even though it would make us more visible. "It will do us no good if she catches pneumonia," he said. Myra and Irina seemed relieved that he suggested the fire. Perhaps they would have insisted on it if he hadn't.

Once during the night, I awoke suddenly and thought I heard a twig snap. Was something or someone out there? My heart began to pound. But there was no second sound, and I drifted back to sleep.

Suddenly I was awake again, and something was dragging me out of my bedroll. I screamed as loudly as I could, "Help, Jakob! Some animal has me!"

All three of my companions jumped up in a flash. Jakob grabbed a glowing branch from the fire, waving it toward me. Sure enough, I saw Amian's dark eyes glinting at me.

"Stop!" Jakob commanded.

His deep voice stopped Amian, but he stood his ground and didn't let go of me.

"What right have you to take our girl-child?" Jakob demanded.

"She was promised to me."

"No!" I cried. "The chief said you must wait until I am a woman."

"You're a woman now," he leered. "I can vouch for that."

"Yes, you raped me. But that doesn't give you any rights to me."

"Let go of her, before I throttle you," Jakob said, his voice growing even sterner.

We seemed to be at an impasse. Then another figure loomed out of the trees, tall and blond. "Whatever are you up to, Amian?" he asked.

"I want my woman back."

"Your woman?" The figure stepped into the firelight, and this time I knew it was Jon. My heart sank.

"He raped me," I murmured to him, but my voice had nearly lost itself in tears.

"Raina? Is that you?" Jon asked.

"Yes, Jason's sister."

"She can be no older than ten or eleven Standard Years." Jon turned to Amian sounding angry. "Have you become a pedophile here in the Wilds?"

"I can take what I wish!" Amian hissed.

"You seem to forget who's High Chieftain here," said Jon.

Amian grimaced. "Surely, you'll grant your old friend a request," he said slyly.

"Not this one," Jon said, and his voice sounded like cold steel. "She's a friend of mine. I don't want this life for her. You'll only use her, and when she's truly a woman, you'll cast her off, and go for another child. I know your kind." His voice was full of hatred now.

Amian's grip on me was loosening, and as soon as I felt him relax, I jumped out of his grasp and fled to Jakob's arms.

"So, she prefers the old man," sneered Amian.

"He's my protector," I said, looking only at Jon. "Where is Jael?" I asked.

"He's in the High Camp at the base of the Peaks," he replied. "I entrusted him to Daiah."

I heard a gasp from Irina. Now she knew at least one of her sons still lived. "Martina?" she managed to whisper.

"She's there, too," said Jon. Meanwhile, Jon grabbed Amian by the collar of his tunic. "I am taking you back to the Peaks Camp," he said fiercely. "You'll pay for this crime."

"What crime?" Amian whined.

"Shut up, Amian! Once I called you my friend, but you're just scum to me now." Pulling Amian with him, Jon turned to go, then stopped for a moment and looked at Irina. "I'm sorry I can't take you to Jael and Martina. They've been with the Redlarks long enough to forget, so I don't know whether they retain any of their memories. Besides, it would be better if you and your friends arrive without me."

Then the two of them disappeared back into the forest. We could hear their voices for awhile, and then only a few dislodged stones clattering sporadically.

Irina took my hand, and I could feel hers quivering. "So that's Jon."

I nodded. "He was always unpredictable, but he and my brother were friends."

"Jakob, do you know how to find this camp? The camp where my children are."

"I'm not sure. But I'll do my best, Irina."

"But I thought we were going to find Dominic," I said. "I'd like to see Jael, too. But I'm afraid to go where Amian is."

Irina took my hand. "We won't let him harm you again, Raina."

Jakob stood for a long time after he built our breakfast fire. I could tell he was thinking about what we should do. After we ate, he and Myra talked softly while Irina and I cleaned up the breakfast things.

Finally, when everything was packed, Irina asked, "Well, where are we going first?"

"If we head for the Peaks, we may pass Jon's camp on our way to Dominic's safe house," said Myra. "There are no guarantees."

"I understand," sighed Irina. "Did you find information about where this safe house is?"

"Yes, there was a cipher in the cave. We must find Dominic if we are to get off-planet," Jakob added. "That will be the safest thing for Raina. You don't realize what happens in these camps. Most of The People are deep into drugs, and evil spirits."

"Well, that explains why Amian is such a beast," Irina said. "Let's head for Dominic if we must. I'll hope we find Jon's camp, too, if we're meant to." I could tell she was upset about this and reached for her hand. "I will leave it in the Lord's hands, whether I see my children again," she sighed.

CHAPTER 6

TREK TO THE PEAKS

Those jagged peaks were looming closer each day. Some days the sun was blinding as it reflected off the snowfields above us. Jakob said some of the largest patches were rivers of ice called glaciers.

The mountains were stunning, but they also scared me, like an obstacle we'd never be able to cross. I remembered how Jael often stood with me on Neptune Spire, looking out at these peaks, watching the sunset. He said they looked like the edge of the world. Right now, I was wondering if we'd ever get to that edge, and what we'd see if we did.

Occasionally, I heard Myra and Jakob whispering to each other as we trekked, apparently trying to decide what to do. I knew Irina wanted desperately to see Jael and Martina, but Jakob felt we should find Dominic first. Myra seemed to be caught in the middle of these two opinions.

It wasn't hard to imagine how Irina felt. If I had a chance to find Jason or my parents, I'd want to do that first, too, but I'd given up any hope of finding my family. No one we'd met since our flight from the City seemed to know anything about them. It would have been hard enough to have this aching empty place in my heart, but now there was the great fear of being retaken by Amian, overshadowing everything else. I just wanted to find Dominic and get away from Terres as soon as possible.

After many days—I lost count since I didn't have a stick to cut notches in—we came into a broad green valley at the very base of the Peaks. There were several huts scattered across the fields, but no one seemed to be living in them. It was eerie to see all these empty dwellings.

"I wonder where they've gone," said Myra.

No one bothered to answer her because we didn't know, either.

Jakob made his decision then and turned away from the valley. He took a narrow trail that led off to the left of the highest mountain. My pack-sack seemed to be getting heavier again, but I kept on, not wanting to be a complainer. We made our camp in the shelter of some scraggly shrubs that night.

"I don't want us to be seen before we can see who's coming," said Jakob.

"Where exactly are we heading?" Irina asked.

"We will follow this trail up to that pass," he replied,

pointing to a low section of the range above us. "Dominic's safe house is there."

I heard Irina sigh and knew what she was thinking. The decision had been made.

Early the next morning, we set out again. The trail was getting steeper with each step, and I got to where all I could do was watch my feet and force them to take one more step. My eyes rarely looked up to see the steep grandeur above us. All I could do was will myself to keep going.

The sun was high overhead when Jakob finally stopped, and we collapsed onto some boulders alongside the trail. Irina and I were too tired to speak. Myra looked like she was more used to this sort of thing, and Jakob really surprised me with how well he was doing. I began to wonder if he was really as old as he looked. Perhaps this 'old man' was just a disguise. After all, if they were Rebels, they'd need to find such ways to hide their true identities. I even began to wonder if Jakob was really Myra's father.

After eating a small snack of some dried berries Myra pulled from her pack, we each took a swig from the water-carrier and pulled ourselves up to our feet again.

The trail continued to climb, and my feet continued to move. My mind was numb, and all I could think about was taking my next breath, listening to the pounding of my heart.

Suddenly, Jakob stopped and put his hand in the air,

motioning for us to hide behind some scrubby trees just off the trail.

Above us, I heard clattering gravel, like someone was running. We crouched down as low as we could, hoping we wouldn't be seen. Then a young woman dressed in blue came within arm's length of me, running fast, and breathing hard. She went on past without a pause. I was about to step back onto the trail when I heard a shout above me.

"Beata, wait!"

Then another figure dashed past us, but I couldn't tell if it was a man or woman. After this, we stayed in our hiding places for a while longer. When no other sounds were coming from above us, Jakob finally motioned for us to begin walking again.

"What was that about?" Myra asked.

Jakob shrugged. "They seemed upset, but I have no idea what it means."

After going only a short distance on the trail, however, he veered off. Now the going was even more difficult, as we stepped over rocks and roots, trying to avoid stepping into any holes. I'd thought I was tired before, but I was wrong.

At last, we reached the top of the saddle-shaped swale that Jakob called the pass. Now we could begin to pick our way down through the boulders and scrub-brush. This was not much easier, but at least I started to catch my breath, now that we weren't climbing. Still, I was afraid I might slip and slide down some of the steep rocky slopes.

When we reached a level area, I felt a great sense of relief. Now Jakob veered off to the right, toward what looked like a large pile of boulders. As we got closer, I could see these rocks were the size of houses. There seemed to be a crack in one of the largest ones, and we were heading directly toward it. Myra now took the lead, and as soon as she reached this crack, she turned sideways and squeezed herself into it. Each of us followed.

As I made my way into the gap between the rocks, with Irina close behind me, I was surprised to find that we were in a cave. The sound of dripping water came to my ears, and once my eyes adjusted to the dimmer light, I began to see a makeshift table made of a boulder with smaller rocks around it acting as chairs. Seated on one of these chairs was a tall blond man.

Irina gasped. "Steph?"

The man rose to his feet. "I'm Dominic, his twin. You look familiar."

Irina grabbed my hand, gripping me so tightly that it hurt. "You look so much like my late husband," she sighed. "And I haven't seen you, Dominic, since—since you left the City."

"Irina? No, how can it be you? Yet you do look so much like my Karina who died, along with our second baby," he sighed.

"She was my twin sister." Irina was weeping openly now. "How could I forget her so soon?"

"You were captive in the Institute, remember?" I whispered to her.

Meanwhile, the man rose and moved quickly toward her. "So it is you, Irina! I haven't seen you for so long. Please, don't cry. Karina knew how much you cared," he said. "Perhaps I'm the most to blame—I took her from the City to live in this wild, uncivilized place."

"No one is to blame, Dominic."

"Please, come sit with me, Irina," he whispered.

Myra stepped quickly to her side and guided Irina toward the circle of rocks. "Remember," she whispered, "All our loved ones are with the Lord, and we *will* see them waiting for us there when our time comes."

"I hope so," she sighed.

As the four of us found rocks to sit on, Dominic seated Irina closest to him. "It's so good to see you again," he said, nodding to Jakob. "How are you, my old friend?"

"I'm well," Jakob said. "As is Myra."

"It's also good to see you, Myra. And as you heard, I haven't seen Irina for many, many years," he said. "I was so sorry to hear of my twin brother's death—and felt very guilty I couldn't be there for you."

Irina didn't seem to have any voice but just nodded. I kept trying to see if there were any tears in her eyes.

"This is Raina," Myra said. "We found her as she

and Irina fled the disaster in Terres-City. Unfortunately, the Redlark who was our guide took a liking to her and molested her."

Dominic looked at me, and I saw a sparkle in his green eyes. "She needs our help, then."

"Yes sir," said Myra.

Irina suddenly spoke, "Our firstborn son, Stephen, is also dead!" And now she broke down into sobs.

I tried to hug her, but I was on a smaller rock, and couldn't reach high enough. Instead, I laid my head on her lap. As Irina reached down and began to smooth my tangled hair, I could feel the gentleness in her touch.

"Our girl-child has been good for Irina," Myra whispered.

"I can see that," said Dominic. He reached for Irina's hand and took it gently in his. "I *have* received word about your youngest child, Irina."

'Of Jael?' I thought. I was afraid to ask whether this news was good or bad.

"First, though, we must get you some proper food," he said. "You all look famished."

I hadn't realized how hungry I was until I had a bowl of something hot in my hands. It was gone in almost an instant, and a young man, who appeared to be Dominic's helper, filled it for me again.

After we ate, we were shown to a low-ceilinged room, where sleeping mats were spread on the floor. I barely remember lying down. I must have fallen asleep on my way to the mat.

***

I heard voices talking when I awoke, and Irina's bed beside me was empty. Then I recognized her voice and Dominic's, "I'm sorry, Irina. I kept trying to make contact with Martina, but she was always in the High Chieftain's hut or the Temple Pavilion."

"Who is this Daiah you talked about?"

"I've sent for her. Perhaps she can clarify what's happened. I've never seen The People—as the Redlarks call themselves—in such confusion."

I decided to keep lying quietly so I could hear more. Perhaps I'd learn something about Jael's whereabouts.

There were shuffling sounds, and then a quiet female voice joined in, "My name is Daiah, madam. I was taking care of your son after Jon won the Duel and became High Chieftain."

"Jon? Yes, we met him. He's Amian's friend."

"I wouldn't exactly call them friends," Daiah's voice said. "Amian first brought Jon to The People, but it was under false pretenses. Jon thought he would be able to learn to cross the GAP with us."

"So Amian lied to him? Why am I not surprised?" Irina's voice became more high-pitched as she grew angrier.

"Where is Jael now, Daiah?" Dominic asked.

"I don't know. We called him Stel, after the double-star that came just before he joined us. He ran away from our camp, even before we moved for the Ritual of the Mother."

"Where could he go?"

"All I know is Jon and Indril, who was his Consort, have disappeared, too," Daiah said at last.

"Indril?" Irina asked. "I thought Jon said Martina was with him."

"Perhaps that was her City-name. I don't know."

"And now they've disappeared?" Irina's voice was getting higher still.

"They began the Ritual as is always done, and went inside the Pavilion. But when the two days were over, they were nowhere to be found. No one knows what happened to them." Now Daiah's voice was filled with panic, as well. "All The People are in disarray. Our High Chieftain and his Consort have disappeared, and no one knows what to do."

I could hear Irina beginning to fight back sobs again.

"Irina, this doesn't mean they're dead," I heard Dominic say. "They tell me Jon brought Jael with him when he came back to the Redlarks from the City. It could be Jon has taken both Jael and Martina with him on another journey."

"But why?"

"The spirits were giving Stel some torment," Daiah said quietly. "Perhaps it will be better for him to go away with Jon. And Indril—uh, Martina, too. She seemed to be in some sort of trance most of the time."

Now I could hear Irina crying loudly. "Oh, my dear children! How could I have abandoned you?"

"You did *not* abandon them," said Dominic.

Irina didn't reply but continued to sob. I found my heart breaking and got up, in spite of myself. Soon, I was nestling close to her and trying to help wipe away her tears.

"Look now," came Dominic's voice softly, "You have another child who needs you. And I *do* know where Darien is."

"You do?" she gasped.

"Yes, but he's on a secret mission, so I mustn't reveal it just yet."

"So Darien is alive?"

"Yes, and he's joined the Rebels. He's now a follower of the True King."

"What a blessing!" she sighed. "Darien was always so moody and difficult, and yet here he is, on the right path at last."

"You mustn't despair, Irina," he said. "The Lord may have plans for Jael and Martina, too. Just keep on trusting."

I looked over at Daiah and thought how her voice fit her well. She spoke softly, and she looked soft and gentle, with dark wavy hair, and bright blue eyes. When I caught her eye, she smiled at me.

"They say you're a friend of Jael's."

I nodded.

"He misses you," she said, still smiling. "He didn't know whether you survived the inferno of the City. I hope someday he gets to see you again."

Now it was my turn to hold back tears. I'd been so consumed by what happened to me with Amian, I forgot how much I wanted to find Jael.

"What should we do now, Dominic?" Irina asked. "We really need to get away from Terres, for Raina's sake. I just wish we didn't have to leave my children behind."

"Jon is firstborn," said Daiah suddenly. "Perhaps they'll get away, too."

Dominic gave a short whistle. "I didn't realize that. Perhaps it *is* something Jon would do, from what I've heard of him."

"He seemed very forceful when we met him," said Irina.

"That's for sure," I added. "When he used to visit my brother Jason in the City, they talked and argued a lot. Jon seemed to know how to get things done in ways no one else could."

We all lapsed into silence for a few minutes, each with our own thoughts. Then Dominic finally spoke, "I think you all should come with me to the Centauri Sector. There's a battle brewing there. It's also close to Maia, Mother Earth. Most Rebels seem to be moving in that direction. In fact, I've heard my son Donmal is there."

"You mean Maia isn't just a myth?" I asked.

"Of course not! You must have been in a System school," said Dominic. "They've tried very hard to erase Earth from all memories and records."

"But why, sir?"

"To keep better control of our minds, I guess." Then he jumped suddenly to his feet. "Come on, we need to get going. Daiah, it's time for you to choose. Are you going back to The People, or coming with us?"

"I miss my friends who used to live with me, both Jon and Jael. I want to try to find them, so yes, I'll come with you."

CHAPTER 7

THE ROUTE TO ALPHA CENTAURI

I never in my wildest dreams imagined what it was like to cross the GAP. Oh, I heard of the ability only firstborn had to make this jump across space and time. But I'd never been off-planet in my short life.

So here we were, off Terres in the blink of an eye. At least, I think I blinked.

"First, we'll be making a stop on a planet called Platius," Dominic said. "I need to check in with the forward brigade before we actually go to the Centauri Sector."

He was looking at Irina when he said this, so I wondered if there was more to this stop than just 'checking in'. Then he closed his eyes, and in an instant, there was a lone planet orbiting its sun. When he closed his eyes again, we were landing on the planet's surface. It seemed like a miracle.

"Those who aren't firstborn don't feel any shift at all," Myra explained to me. "Only firstborn have any sense of the GAP-crossing. To the rest of us, it seems instantaneous."

"That's a big word," I said. "What does it mean?"

She said this just before we found ourselves sitting in the small spaceport. "Just like that," she smiled. "See? Here we are, and you and I didn't feel a thing."

I just sat, speechless.

***

Now we were in a small house on a remote part of this planet. I was a little disappointed because I hoped to see more of my first 'new planet'. But Myra explained to me that it wasn't safe for us to be seen in the cities on Platius, though she wouldn't say why.

Daiah began to take an interest in me since we both knew Jael. She seemed to have a special place in her heart for him, and I tried not to let any jealousy rise in me over this. We were both listening to Myra with great interest, since this was Daiah's first time off Terres, too.

"This is a Rebel Safe House," Myra continued. "The people here on Platius are a strange lot. In Urbis, they are very strict, and in Colasse they're totally uninhibited, especially on orgy day."

"Orgy day? What's that?"

"Well, Raina," she smiled slightly, "It's a lot like a Redlark Camp, anything goes."

I could tell by the tone of her voice that she meant lots of sex and perversion, so I didn't ask anymore. I had enough of that with Amian.

Just then, Dominic entered the room where we lounged on low cushions. It felt good to get out of the chairs we were strapped into for the crossing.

"I'm sorry, Irina," he said. "It appears Darien has led the first wave of the attack into the Centauri Sector."

I could see she was upset at this, so I went over to her and took her hand. "At least we know he was here."

She merely nodded.

"I'm sure he'll be fine," Dominic added. "He's with a command ship, not a small fighter."

"It seems we always arrive a step behind," Irina sighed at last. "First on Terres and now here."

"But we *are* on the right track," Myra added.

"Yes, we know that, at least," said Dominic. "So, we'll head for the Centauri Sector, too—as soon as I finish my briefing with the Rebel contingent that's still here."

We were only there for a few more hours, so I decided to help Myra and Daiah prepare some food for us to eat before we set off again. There wasn't much variety in the packaged meals we found in the pantry.

"They must not eat very well here," sighed Daiah. "This stuff looks really bland."

"I think it's from Urbis," Myra said. "They don't want anyone to actually enjoy eating."

"Why not?" I asked.

"I'm told they consider any bodily pleasure to be evil, even eating."

"That's really strange!" I said.

Anyway, we had a meal—such as it was—prepared for Jakob and Dominic when they returned.

They seemed to be upset about something, though.

We all gobbled the food and tried not to ask too many questions.

"This stuff is really blah," Jakob commented as we were finishing.

"Yeah, we're sorry," said Myra. "It's from Urbis, we think."

"Well that explains it," Dominic sighed.

Finally, when we finished with the cleanup and put what food was left into pack-sacks to take on the next leg of our journey, Myra managed to get Jakob alone in the galley for a few moments. I hung around nearby, my curiosity roused.

"What is Dominic upset about?" she whispered.

"Some of the Rebels here aren't certain of our time calculations," Jakob replied. "Darien and his wave were certain the Final Battle was imminent, but others don't think so."

"You mean the End of the Age?" There was hushed awe in her voice as she spoke these words.

"That's what Darien and his people think. But The Book does remind us, 'No man knows the day or the hour, but only the Father in Heaven'."

"What does Dominic think?"

"He tends to agree with Darien."

"But you don't?" she asked.

"I don't want to jump to conclusions." Jakob shrugged. "I told Dominic to proceed with caution. But he insists on heading for Alpha Centauri immediately."

"Let's pray the Lord will keep us in the palm of his hand," she whispered.

Then they joined hands, the way I'd often seen them do before, but this time they didn't say words out loud. I was still mystified about this praying stuff. First, they talked aloud to someone who was invisible, and now they just 'thought' to this unseen thing, whatever it was.

***

Now we were all back in the spherical ship, belted into our respective launch chairs. Each one was a different color, so we'd always use the same one, something to do with the G-force and adapting to our size and weight. All I knew about the G-force was it felt like a heavy weight sitting on my chest when we left the planet's surface.

I watched as Dominic closed his eyes, seated in the gold chair with access to the control console. Then we were out in space, looking back at the small orb that was Platius. Again, I felt a thrill of excitement. It was still a wonder to me to be off the surface of a planet.

Myra smiled at me as she noticed my wide-eyed gaze at the now-receding star, Platius' sun.

Then Dominic put new coordinates into the console and nodded to Jakob. "Next stop Alpha Centauri," he said, as he closed his eyes.

I closed my eyes, too, trying to imagine the crossing I couldn't feel.

Suddenly the ship gave a violent lurch.

I was thankful for the straps of my chair because without them I would've been thrown out of it. An explosion of heat seemed to jump out of the view screen above the console.

"What is it?" I heard Myra shout.

"Photo-explosives!" Jakob's voice seemed far away.

Now I could see Dominic slumped over the console.

"Quick!" shouted Jakob. "Help me move him, so I can take the controls."

In a flash, Myra and Jakob managed to pull Dominic's still body into Jakob's chair. Then Jakob took over the pilot's chair and placed his hands on the console, as Dominic did when we first started our journey.

"There," he said, "I'm imprinted now."

"Where should we go?" Daiah asked.

I continued to sit, speechless, my heart pounding.

"First, away from this battle," Jakob said tensely. He closed his eyes.

The flashes of explosions disappeared from the viewer. Instead, a small planet floated into our view.

"Is that Beta or Proxima?" I heard Myra ask. Neither

name meant anything to me.

"I think it's Beta," he replied. "I just chose coordinates with medical facilities."

"Yes, we need them first," she nodded.

And then, in another blink of my eyes, we were on the surface of this planet. It appeared Jakob took us to a spaceport this time. I hoped we wouldn't be in trouble in this place.

"Is it safe here?" Daiah asked, voicing my fears.

"It's a Rebel outpost," Jakob said. "We can get medical help for Dominic."

The next thing I knew, our airlock opened and in stepped two men in long jackets. Between them, they carried a litter.

"Here," said Irina. She'd been staying close to Dominic's still body, in total silence since the explosion. "He's been shocked by a photo-explosion." I could tell she was afraid he would die like his twin brother—her husband.

The men gently moved Dominic onto their stretcher and carried him through the airlock. The rest of us rose to follow them.

***

The five of us were seated in a waiting area—Irina, Myra, Jakob, Daiah, and me—staring at each other or the floor. The waiting seemed like hours for any news on

Dominic's condition. I felt a deep ache in the pit of my stomach, and there was nothing I could do about it. Even though I hadn't known him as long as the rest of them, he'd become dear to me because of—well, I couldn't really put it into words—just because of who he was.

His way of smiling at you made you feel loved and warm inside, and this seemed to come to everyone who knew him, not just relatives and close friends. Yet, he also was a strong leader. People respected his judgment and followed his orders and advice. To me, he seemed like a beloved uncle or perhaps even a father, and I suddenly realized having Dominic around was taking away some of the pain of losing my family.

"I just can't bear to lose him," I heard myself say.

Irina took my hand. That was when I realized I actually spoke my thoughts aloud.

"All of us hold him dearly," she said. "He's a wonderful man."

"Is he much like your husband, his brother?" Myra asked.

"In many ways, yes. My Steph wasn't as vocal about his feelings as Dominic is. He was a more private person, but he still had the same warmth that drew people to him."

Jakob stood suddenly and began to pace the small room.

Myra put her hands over her face, trying to hide her tears.

Just then, a figure in white entered the waiting area. We all looked up expectantly but fearfully.

"He's very strong," said the doctor. "It will be a long recuperation, but he'll live."

Each of us heaved a deep sigh.

"Is he allowed visitors yet?" asked Daiah.

"Only one at a time."

At this, all of us looked at Irina. "You should go first," said Jakob. "You're the only true relative here."

Irina's eyes showed how grateful she was to hear this. "May I?"

The doctor nodded and took her with him through the swinging doors.

While she was gone, the rest of us found our minds could function again, now that we'd heard good news.

"Has there been any word of Darien?" Myra asked.

"I've also heard he went with the first wave," said Jakob. "I talked briefly with one of the Rebel leaders at this port. Darien's ship was attacked by the Colassenes and had to take evasive action. No one knows for sure where they ended up, but the last communication showed them on a path for Maia—Mother-Earth."

"Really?" asked Daiah. "I thought Maia was just a myth."

"I did, too," I said, smiling at her.

"Oh no. It's very real, despite all the System's efforts to erase it from the records," said Myra.

"There was also a communication about some unusual stowaways on Darien's ship, but nothing was ever clarified," Jakob added.

I found myself wondering whether Earth would be any different from Terres, but didn't say anything. Instead, I just hoped we might find Darien so Irina could be with at least one of her children.

Then I decided to take a walk in the corridors near the waiting area, and Daiah said she'd join me.

"How long have you been a Redlark?" I asked, just for something to say as we walked.

"Probably since I was about your age," she smiled. "I ran away from home because my father was abusive."

"Did he—uh—rape you?" I found this word was always in the front of my mind these days.

"No, but he beat my mother and me. I couldn't get her to leave him, though. I don't know what happened to her."

"Why didn't you forget this? I thought everyone who came to the Redlarks forgot their past."

"Most do," she sighed. "But I guess some of my memories were too awful to forget. I wish I *had* forgotten them."

I was silent, trying to think of what to say. At last, I said, "I don't know what happened to my family after the disaster."

"Then we have something in common," she sighed.

"That's why I hope someday I can find Jael," I whispered.

"Me, too. He's a special person, isn't he?"

"How long did he live with you, Daiah?"

"I'm not sure of the time. It seems like it was a couple of seasons. I taught Jael how to hunt and boat on the river."

"I would've liked to learn those things, too," I said. "So how long have you known Dominic?"

"I met him several years ago when he was living in our camp. He ran from the City, you know, and was declared non-existent by the Council. He even brought his family with him."

"So they were all cast out."

"Yes, but he didn't seem to be able to forget his past either. Then he and his family went to find the Rebels. Jon and Jael's memories stayed with them, too. Maybe it runs in the family."

She stopped talking then, and we just walked in silence. When we came to a window that looked into a small courtyard between the buildings, we paused for a moment.

"Was it painful?" she asked softly, "When Amian…"

I wanted to look at her but found I couldn't. "Yes, very painful."

She silently took my hand.

"But the mental pain is worse," I added. "I'm not sure what to do about it."

"I know," she said softly. "I was a girl of only twelve Standard Years when he forced himself on me."

I turned to her in surprise. She seemed like such a calm and happy person, not like someone who'd been raped. She must have seen the question in my eyes, for she went on, "You think I don't show it?" There was a hint of a smile in her voice.

I found I could only nod.

"You can't always tell what a person carries inside by what you see on their face."

"What did you do to get past it?" I finally managed to ask.

She put her arm around my shoulders. "Time will help," she sighed. "And you can always feel free to talk to me."

I was crying into her shoulder by this time. "Thank you, Daiah. It's good to know that you understand." I couldn't finish what I wanted to say then, but she kept hugging me and let me cry as long as I needed to.

At last, stepping back, I took a deep breath and tried to wipe away my tears. Daiah smiled at me, and said, "Jael often talked of the True Lord his family believed in, Raina. He sounds like he's powerful and loving. Perhaps when we find Jael, he can help you with this pain."

"If we find Jael."

"I bet if he were here, he'd tell us to keep our hopes up. You know, that feier-cat of his often said such things, when I could hear his thoughts.”

“Feier? He was with Jael?”

“Yes, all the time he was in the Camp. The Priests didn’t like it, but they feared Feier and left him alone.”

“Thanks, Daiah. You *have* given me hope. If Jael still has Feier, I think he’ll be okay. Did you know I gave Feier to him as a present?”

“That was you? He talked about a dear friend who gave him the feier-cat, but I had no idea it was you. If he did mention your name, I forgot.”

We were staring at each other now in surprise. To think we both had a special place in the same person’s life seemed to bring us closer together. I reached out and slipped my arm through Daiah’s.

“I’m glad that I’ve met you, Daiah.”

“Same here, Raina.”

***

When we got back to the waiting room, Jakob had gone in to see Dominic, and Irina was telling Myra what they’d talked about.

“He thinks they’ll send him to Maia as soon as he’s strong enough to travel. His son is there.”

“Didn’t Jakob say they thought Darien’s ship was headed to Maia?”

Irina nodded.

"So perhaps we'll catch up with some of your family yet," Myra smiled.

"They seem so elusive," Irina shrugged. "Always one step ahead of us."

I settled myself into the seat next to Irina. It had begun to feel natural to think of her as my new mother. As soon as I joined her, she took my hand. Perhaps she was starting to think of me as a daughter, too.

"I have Raina," she said then. "So I'm never completely alone." She smiled at me, and I felt a warmth begin to spread inside me.

Squeezing her hand, I whispered, "I love you, Irina."

Her eyes began to tear up. "I love you, too, Raina."

***

The days and weeks went by, and we stayed in lodgings in the barracks with the Rebels there on Beta Centauri. Finally, the doctors pronounced Dominic safe for travel. Since he couldn't cross the GAP himself yet, a former Star Corps pilot was assigned to us. Jakob was firstborn, too, but said he preferred a more experienced pilot than himself.

I grew very excited at the thought of actually seeing Earth, a place I always believed merely mythical. Would it be like other planets? Or completely different? What was it that made it so special? To the Rebels, it was almost sacred, and to the System, it was so forbidden that they'd tried to erase it from all human minds and records.

"Why is Earth so important?" I finally asked Myra one day, as we were packing gear for the trip.

"Well, it's where all mankind originally came from, Raina. And it's where the Lord of the Universe was actually born into time, as a human."

"I'm sure not exactly sure what all this means. I hope it will make more sense to me when I get there."

"I'm sure it will," she smiled and patted my arm.

The next morning, we were each in our respective chairs in launch position. I checked my restraining harness three times. I was so excited and nervous. On my left was Daiah, and on my right was Irina. Dominic was in a special bed adapted for the flight, with Myra and Jakob on either side of him.

Then, the pilot nodded to each of us. "Prepare yourselves for lift-off." I saw him close his eyes, and knew that he was concentrating on the coordinates that so few knew anymore, the coordinates that would take us to Maia.

And soon, there it was—all swirls of blue and white, looking like it was mostly water.

["Wow!" said Ginna. "I can see it, just as you saw it, Raina. Even though I'm not even 'inside' Martina right now."

"It really is amazing looking, isn't it?" Martina replied.

"I've seen pictures from our NASA spaceships, but the real thing is so much, well, just more," Danny added.

"So what happens now?" Ginna asked. "Can we go back to your story, Martina?"

Jon was giving her that 'look' again. "Not yet, Ginna."

"You two need to stay in your own time for a little while," said Martina.

Martina's voice was fading now—like a lonely train whistle echoing into the distance.

Suddenly, Ginna knew the others were gone. In desperation, she grabbed her brother's hand. "Where did they go?" she cried.

"I don't know."

"How do you feel, Danny?"

"Sort of empty, Sis."

"Me too. I feel like there's no point to this life here, without Jon—oh, and Martina."

Danny gave her a sharp look. "Do you think maybe you're getting too attached to Jon?"

She shook her head. "It's just that I've been feeling what Martina does for him. Don't worry, I'll be all right." Even as she said this, she was telling herself deep inside to try to make these words come true.

Then she realized they were sitting back on their old couch.

"I guess we go on from where we left off?" Danny shrugged.

"Yeah, I wonder if it's a school day or a weekend?"

"If it's like last time, it's the same day we left."

So they walked into the kitchen, and Mom still wasn't home yet.

CHAPTER 8

GINNA PARKER

She woke up feeling depressed. Another dream about Mom and Dad, and this one seemed all too real. She shook her head, but it wouldn't leave her mind. Looking around in confusion, she realized she must have fallen asleep on the couch doing homework. Books were still piled around her, though a couple were on the floor.

Where was Danny? Then she remembered. He was at his friend Justin's for a sleep-over. She hated being home alone. Why wasn't Mom home yet?

Just then a ring-tone jolted her out of her drowsiness. Groping through the pile of books and papers, she finally found her cell phone between the couch cushions.

"Hello?"

"Ginna, it's Mom."

"What's up?"

"I'll be working late again, Honey. I'm sorry."

"With John Cameron, I suppose?"

"Yes, of course. Is that a problem?" There was a quick sharpness in Mom's voice.

"No, Mom." She wanted to say 'yes', but what was the point?

"You'll probably be asleep when I get home."

"Yeah, sure. 'Bye, Mom."

"'Bye, Honey."

Ginna sighed as she hung up the phone. So Mom was having an affair. That seemed pretty clear. Not that she hadn't suspected. After all, she wasn't born yesterday.

'I just don't want Mom to get hurt again,' she thought.

She understood how her mother still felt the pain of the divorce. But why couldn't she find someone closer to her own age, someone who wasn't already married? The more she thought about it, the angrier she got. 'Mom is letting this man take advantage of her, just because she's been devastated by the divorce.'

Now she let her mind drift back to the memories she dreaded. Maybe if she could just think of them as bad dreams, they'd eventually fade away.

Lauren Graves, her mother, had met Tim Parker in high school in Houston, Texas. They'd married shortly after starting college. Had they really been in love, or were they too young when they married?

'I have a boyfriend now,' Ginna thought. 'But I think I'm too young to really be in love. Is that what happened to Lauren and Tim? I know from being 'in' Martina that I don't have the kind of feelings she has for Jon.

'Did Mom really have those deep feelings for Dad? They must have been happy once. But what is falling in love, anyway? And why do so many people fall out of it?

'I guess I can understand Mom feeling like she needs to get even with Dad. But is this affair the way to do it? I shouldn't be in this position, having to lecture my own mother on morality. It should be the other way around. But maybe it's better to say what I think and get criticized for it. The other way—if I don't say what I feel—I may wish later that I did.'

So, with a sigh, she decided to tell Mom how she really felt and got out her cell phone to send a text:

"Mom, don't think u'll get back at Dad this way. U're the one who'll get hurt."

But after she sent the text, she found she couldn't get her mind off the divorce, which came when she was thirteen. The angry words echoed through their house in her mind:

"I've found someone else, Lauren. I'm sorry."

"You bastard! Why? Wasn't I good enough for you? Wasn't it enough that I gave up my career for yours? That I gave you two beautiful children? How can you do this to us?"

"You always talk about what you gave up. Don't you see that makes me feel guilty?"

"Why should you feel guilty? I love you, and I'd do anything for you, Tim."

"The only thing you can do for me now is to let me go free."

"Alright then—go free! Get out of here, and never come back. I don't want to ever see your lying face again."

Of course, Ginna knew they *did* have to see each other again, in divorce court. Each hired a lawyer, to help sort out who got what. Dad got the house, because by that time Mom found this job in Colorado. Mom got custody of her and Danny, and Dad had some visitation rights. But for some reason Ginna didn't understand, he never used them. She and Danny hadn't seen him since the divorce.

Now Ginna found tears sliding down her cheeks. She should be over all this by now. Why did she have to even think about it? Angry with herself, she stomped onto the rickety back porch and looked westward toward the Rocky Mountains looming far away on the horizon.

Once, over five years ago, as she and Danny stood looking at a sunset similar to this one, the two strangers came, Jon and Jael. They were time-travelers from the future, a Parallel Universe, they said. The story they shared was one of finding hope in spite of trials and problems, and it did seem to help Danny somehow. She wasn't sure whether anything would help her with the swirling turmoil of emotions she kept locked inside.

The second time they came, Jael brought his sister,

Martina, with them. Having another girl to talk to helped a lot more.

"I sure could use a visit now," she sighed aloud. "I really miss Martina. But I know they don't come when I *want* them, only when I really need them."

Still, she kept her gaze on the horizon, wishing she could see figures walking toward her, the same as before. Soon, however, the sun dipped behind the Front Range (as Colorado people called it) and the shadows of evening stretched across the open field behind their house.

This little old house on the edge of town was supposed to be temporary—"until we can find something better"—Mom said. But she didn't even bother with saying this anymore. Every time Dad's child support was late or didn't come at all, she'd just shrug and say, "Guess we'll keep on renting for a while."

At last, the sky turned to the purplish shade of twilight, and the first star (which was probably a planet) shone above her. Ginna turned and went toward the door. Suddenly, a figure stepped out of the shadows at the other end of the porch.

She screamed.

"Hey, Ginna," came a strangely familiar voice. "Don't be afraid. After all, you're the one who called me."

"What? I didn't call anyone."

Then, as her eyes adjusted to the dimness on the porch, she began to make out a young woman about her size with long dark hair that fell past her shoulders.

"You did call me," she said calmly.

Ginna stepped back in shock. "Martina, is that really you?"

"Of course it's me."

"I never thought I could call anyone. It seemed like it was always Danny."

"Well I'm here, so you must have."

"I guess. Where are the others?"

"You mean Jael and Jon? Well, they'll get Danny when it's time, and I'm here to take you back."

Ginna could only nod, but in the back of her mind, she was thinking, 'It makes sense that Jael isn't here, since Danny isn't either. He's at a friend's. And maybe Jon didn't come because he thinks I have a crush on him. Okay, I admit I do have a crush on Jon.'

The last time, when all three came, they took Danny and Ginna with them through a time warp to their future time. There she experienced what Martina did, including her beginning to realize her love for Jon. And if she was honest with herself, Ginna knew that she felt envious of Martina having someone like Jon to love her.

"Well, I guess I did call you," she finally said. "So what do we do from here?"

"Let's go inside, okay? I'm getting cold out here."

Ginna smiled at this. Martina must not be used to Colorado nights.

The evenings were cooler here because the dry air didn't hold the heat like it did in more humid places.

Once inside, they sat on the sagging old couch, the same place they'd always begun. Martina got out the strange amber-colored lamp that Jael and Jon used before.

"You know," she said, "I'm not really sure how this works. I'm not firstborn, so I don't have the ability to cross the GAP, but *you* have the potential. Jon told me that with this lamp, you and I can open the passage between our worlds so you can hear the rest of my story. What did you think of Raina's story, by the way?"

"Raina? Oh yeah, gosh I feel sorry for her. She's lost all her family, and then that Amian—Ugh! What's going to happen to her next?"

"We'll get back to her," said Martina, "But first I need to catch you up on some stuff that happened to me."

Ginna just nodded again. Any words she might say were stuck somewhere in her throat now.

Martina lit the lamp, and shades of gold, amber, red, and brown began to swirl around them, illuminating all of the tiny living room. It felt strange to be doing this without Danny.

Then she found she wasn't sitting on the couch anymore. She was outside again, looking toward the mountains, and her voice was speaking, but it was really Martina's.

CHAPTER 9

MOTHER-MAIA

Our touchdown on Maia was fairly uneventful *[Martina's voice was saying]*. Darien even let Jon retake the console. I could tell he was jealous of Jon's ability as firstborn to cross the GAP, but this didn't surprise me.

Darien always was the most temperamental of my three brothers. I knew he envied Stephen, our tall and handsome eldest brother. Stephen was the one with the curly blond hair that the women seemed to like, and he was the one who was a pilot in the Star Corps. But Darien had his music and played manitar very well. Jael and I loved to sit and listen to him when he would let us.

So, at last, we made it to Earth, the place the rest of the Galaxy denied existed. I still can't believe we actually just stumbled onto Darien and his troop, as stowaways on a ship from Platius. It seems unbelievable. But I've seen other things in my short life that would seem incredible, too—like how Jon and Jael somehow managed to find each other and to come for me, when I was lost to the spirits of The People. And I can see Darien has really changed from the confused and angry brother he once was.

But I can also see he's puzzled by what we've found on Earth. There's no visible King. People just come and go like any other place. The only real difference we've found so far is there are still books and writing here, something very rare in the rest of the Galaxy.

I'm hoping we can find this Fountain Johan told us about—the one that can cleanse us of every bad thing we've done. I think that will be the only way I can ever be rid of the things from my past which still haunts me. Oh, I know Jon says he forgives me for all the bad and foolish things I've done. But I feel I need something more, though I don't exactly know what it is.

Often since we got here, Jon has said he loves me and want us to marry, like people used to long ago. "It's a way to show our commitment to each other," he said. "Don't you still believe in the old ways your family taught?"

"I think I do, Jon. But it's a big step, and you know what a weakling I am. I'm afraid I'll let you down."

"You can never let me down, Martina." He took my hand. "I accept you the way you are, strengths and weaknesses."

A lump was tightening in my throat, and tears were trying to seep from my eyes. "I just need more time, Jon, to work through the ghosts of my past."

"That's what you always say," he sighed.

***

"Well, this is Maia," Jon mused, as he looked out the window of our small room.

"Some of it," I nodded. "We saw many different types of terrain, as we came in with Darien's shuttle."

"Does anyone know the name of that city on the horizon?" Jael was pointing toward the hazy skyline of tall buildings we could just make out.

"I heard Darien call it Celeton," I said. I enjoyed looking at the greens and golds of the farm fields around us, more than at the hazy city.

'This is a Rebel Safe House. Darien warned other places here may not be safe for us,' Feier's thought came into my mind. It still took me by surprise to hear him. He'd been Jael's pet for all of our wanderings, but he only recently reached my mind so I could hear him the way Jon and Jael did. Sometimes I wondered if something changed in me so I could hear him now, or had the change been in Feier himself?

"Yes, Darien told us." Jael was rubbing the feier-cat's head in the place he seemed to like best, behind the ears. "I wonder how much longer we have to stay here. It's been weeks."

I was feeling frustrated that all we could do was stand here and talk. I knew it was pointless but decided to express my thoughts aloud, "But how are we ever going to find the Fountain if we can't leave this house?"

"Now, Martina."

"Don't you start, Jon." I was in no mood for another of his 'Be patient' lectures, and yet I felt ashamed of my impatience as soon as I said it.

"Sis, please."

'I believe it's time for me to try my wings,' Feier's thought came softly.

"Your wings!" Jael looked up in surprise. "I forgot you can fly."

"I've never seen him fly," I shrugged.

'Well, up until now I've been too young. But now I've reached the age of fledging.'

"Wow!" mouthed Jael. "But do you think you'll be safe here?"

"I don't see that we have any other options right now," said Jon. "Where will you go, Feier? How far can you fly?"

'I'm not sure yet. I think a flight to scout that city will work, though.'

"Well, if you're willing, we'd appreciate your help." Jon stepped closer to Jael and his pet.

"Yes, but please be careful." Jael put his face close to Feier's.

Feier gave him a quick lick with his rough tongue, catching a tear slipping down Jael's cheek.

'I must start if I expect to be back before dark.' Feier

extended his wings then, a sight we hadn't seen in a long time. The skin of them looked thicker than before, and they seemed to extend almost twice as wide. He'd only used them to scare attackers away before this. Now they *did* seem strong enough to support his weight.

'Farewell, Jael. I'll return as soon as I can.'

"Please come back soon," Jael's voice broke.

***

The rest of that day seemed to drag by. Jael sat and tried to read from The Book, but I often saw him just staring into space. I walked back and forth between him and the window. Jon went into the yard behind the house, venting his energies splitting wood for the fireplace. The steady *thunk, thunk* of the axe became a rhythm to my pacing.

At last, the shadows were lengthening as the sun dropped toward the horizon in the west.

"It sure feels strange to see the sun set in the west, doesn't it, Sis?"

"I know. On Terres, where we lived most of our lives, it *rose* in the west."

"But if this is really mankind's home planet, then there were countless generations of our ancestors who saw the sun rise in the east and set in the west."

"It *is* kind of wonderful to think we had ancestors here, isn't it?"

We lapsed into silence again, not wanting to mention it was getting dark, and Feier wasn't back. The door slammed as Jon came in, laden with a large armload of chopped wood. With a *crash*, he dropped it down next to the hearth.

"Guess I'll start a fire." He knelt and began to arrange the wood.

I was glad he hadn't asked anything about Feier just yet.

Soon a warm fire was crackling in the stone fireplace on one side of the central room of the house. A sudden sound at the door made us all jump and look toward it in anticipation.

The figure that stepped in, however, was Darien.

"Hey, what's up?" He seemed surprised we all were looking at him.

"We were wondering if you might be Feier," I said at last.

"Jael's pet? No, I haven't seen him."

I could see Jael clenching and unclenching his fists as he stared intently out the window. "He'll be back soon. He promised me."

I looked up at Darien and shrugged slightly. "Feier said he'd go to scout the city."

Darien frowned at this news. "I wish you'd wait until I okay this sort of mission."

Jon rose from beside the hearth then. "You may be

the Rebels' leader, but that doesn't mean we have to answer to you for our every thought and move."

"But I do have to think of my people's safety. I won't allow your schemes to jeopardize that."

I stepped between Jon and Darien, hoping to defuse this conversation.

"We're sorry, Dare." I tried to look repentant. "We've been looking for Maia and its Fountain for a very long time. Feier offered to go, and we let him. Please try to understand how important this is to us."

Jon slipped his arm around my waist and pulled me toward him. I felt uneasy at this, wondering if he was just doing this to send a message to my older brother. So I slipped out of his hold and put my hands on Darien's chest.

"I never seem to get a chance to tell you how good it is to see you again," I whispered. Behind me, I could sense Jon stiffening. He seemed to be trying to send me a signal that he wanted to play this game by his rules, not mine. This only made me angrier with him. "I can't tell you how much we've missed you, Darien."

"Really?" His eyes grew wider. "I always thought Stephen was your favorite."

"How can you think I never loved you? We're a family, and I'm so glad the three of us are together again, at last."

Jon made a big show just then of turning and plunking down on a chair beside the fireplace. I was getting weary of all these displays of male ego.

"All right, both of you!" I was suddenly at the end of my rope with the two of them. "Would you just stop with this? Darien, you're my brother, and I love you. Jon, you know I care for you. But what am I supposed to do when you two keep acting like this?"

Neither of them seemed ready to answer me, each staring at the floor at his feet. I found myself almost wanting to laugh. Men were so insecure!

Just then, a wind blew the backdoor open, and along with dry leaves, a small figure with wings entered.

"Feier! Look everyone, he's back!" Jael ran over and picked the feier-cat up. "Are you all right, Feier?"

'Yes, I'm fine. It was farther than I thought to the city. I'm sorry if I caused you to worry.'

"We're just glad you *are* back," I sighed.

"Did you find out anything interesting?" Jon couldn't resist being the first to ask.

"Let's all sit down by the hearth." I pulled Darien with me over to where Jon was sitting.

They managed to sit on either side of me and avoid looking at each other. Jael nestled at Jon's side with Feier on his lap. I reflected Darien didn't seem as worried about Jon's attention toward Jael as he did about the attention toward me. I smiled to myself, thinking about how it *was* nice to have an older brother looking out for me again.

Jael stroked Feier gently for a few minutes. "He needs to catch his breath."

Jon stoked the fire again, adding two more logs. Soon they were snapping and popping as the flames licked their sides. I liked to watch the way the yellow flames curled around each timber. There always seemed to be something fascinating about a fire.

'I flew all the way to where the great city reaches the banks of a wide river,' Feier began.

I wondered if Darien could hear him, but he didn't say anything, so I guessed this meant he did. Perhaps Feier *was* the one who controlled who heard his thoughts.

'I saw many people and tall buildings but no sign of a fountain, I'm afraid.'

Everyone sighed at this, so I knew each of us heard the feier-cat's thoughts.

"Did you see signs of Rebels preparing for battle?" Darien asked.

'No. Everyone seemed to go about their own business.'

"Perhaps we haven't come into the right time, after all," sighed Darien. "It's so hard to calculate these things, with the GAP Factors and the Relativity Effect."

"Well, I guess we'll just have to stay here a while longer," I said, trying not to sound too gloomy.

Jon didn't say anything. Meanwhile, I was hoping we'd soon be able to find a place of our own because it wasn't going to work having him and Darien living in the same house much longer.

CHAPTER 10

THREE YEARS LATER - THE VALLEY

The sun was just rising over the mountains to the east, causing their jagged silhouettes to stand out starkly, as if on the edge of the world. This image came to me often, remembering Jael's fascination for the mountains of Terres. But just now I was forcing myself not to look too long at these mountains of Earth, lest I drive my old groundcar out of its path. Still, I kept glancing at them from the corner of my eye.

My mind jumped from scene to scene as I remembered the many ways I'd seen these mountains in the past couple of years—hanging aloof and distant in a hot haze, angry and gray with clouds thrown about their shoulders, crisp and white on a clear winter day, the snow shining and making them seem so close I felt I could reach out and touch them—and now with the red and orange hints of sun reaching out from behind them to shatter the deep blue-violet of night.

It was strange to think we'd stayed here on Earth for over three years already. Darien was so sure when we arrived that it was time for the Final Battle. He was ready to take a stand for the True King, then and there. But we'd discovered the Lord has his own timing, not revealed to anyone. And so, we'd found a place to settle in this wide valley between the Modox Mountains and the desert.

We lived among flat farm fields and rolling hills with timber. It wasn't easy getting used to a rural-agricultural culture, something none of us had experienced before. Mostly we'd lived in bustling cities, except for the short time with the Redlarks in the Wilds of Terres.

Jon was happy to find a job working with the timber-cutters. Now we could have financial support of our own. Darien, however, returned to the city of Celeton, a day's journey away by groundcar.

I suspected the rural life here brought back distant memories for Jon of his early life on Rubicon. Thus, the adjustment came more easily for him than for me. This was a good place for Jael in the warm season, too. He worked in our garden and the fields with our neighbors, learning the ways of the land. The three of us kept a large garden in the summer, and it was good to work together to help feed ourselves from its harvest.

But in the cold season, usually seven months long here, Jael couldn't take the bitter cold and the almost-constant winds. I think his body had lost some of its vigor, with the injuries he received when our ship crashed on Platius. Although this was nearly four Standard Years ago, there were still times when exhaustion overcame him.

So I was the one who suggested he spend the long winters in Celeton with Darien. For one thing, Jon felt guilty about the crash, and Jael was a constant reminder of the consequences. But the reason I gave aloud was Jael could attend a better school in Celeton. Besides, he and Darien needed to get to know one another better. Still, it was lonely without him around, and the chill of the long snowy winters seemed to penetrate deep into my soul sometimes.

One thing I noticed, though, was how many memories of my childhood were coming back now. Perhaps it was finding Darien which helped the most. Being around him seemed to awaken some of my old self that I'd lost while I with the Redlarks, back on planet Terres, our old home.

The peace and isolation of the Valley probably helped, too—there was more time to think, and life was more relaxed than before. But I must admit sometimes it was too quiet. So there were forces that seemed to pull me out of this Valley, for although I loved this beautiful place and the quiet simple life it provided for us, there was still a restlessness deep inside me.

In winter, the people of the Valley turned from

their snow-covered farm fields to the deep green forests blanketing the hills around us. While Jon worked in the timber-lands, I took a job as a Terminal Transcriber in the office that coordinated many of the forest activities. It was a rather lowly job, but it was better than nothing. And by making it known I had other talents than scribing and filing, I managed to be chosen for a special assignment in Salien, the city where the forestry manager's office was.

I found it quite ironic that now I was working with a Terminal, the very thing my parents had forbidden in our house. Fortunately, this one—being on Earth—was not strictly controlled by any council or planetary system.

Since Salien was only about four hours away by groundcar, it was slightly closer than Celeton and in another direction. Jon seemed to support me in my hopes to improve my career status, so he didn't complain when I'd have to stay at lodgings in Salien for a couple of weeks. So far we seemed to have a give-and-take relationship, one where neither did all the giving or all the taking. But we were still new at living together, just the two of us.

Now we were approaching the end of my big project, a survey of public opinions on allocation of lands, something always controversial on a planet with a large population and diminishing resources. Though the Valley was sparsely populated, this wasn't the norm, and areas with overflowing populations were looking enviously at what we had.

Many of the resource managers were desperately trying to keep some lands from being overrun by Earth's over-population, but it was a difficult battle. Thus, our project to sort all these demands and opinions seemed very important. The hope was a compromise could be reached as to which areas should be preserved for the future and which should be developed now. And I must admit, I relished the feeling my work was important.

So, I thought back on the events of the past few weeks, the excitement of a challenging task, the responsibility I carried, the knowledge that when I spoke, people listened with respect—for I knew my subject. It had been very gratifying, and I smiled to myself now, remembering.

As I continued the drive, climbing gradually out of the Valley and approaching the outskirts of Salien, I tried to sort some of these feelings out again. I knew I'd come a long way from the girl I was on Terres, always seeking satisfaction with any man who'd have me. Yet now, it was as though the past was coming back to haunt me. Suddenly, it was much too easy to look at other men in ways I felt I should only look at Jon.

At least now the Resource Project was nearly finished, and most of the workers had gone back to their homes. There were just a few finishing touches to put on the report the Project Manager asked me to write. This would be my last trip to Salien.

I arrived in the city with just enough time to check

into the hotel, grab a bite of lunch, and get to the first meeting. Just like the weeks before, the hotel seemed very familiar now. I was confident and comfortable in my work here, and again felt the satisfaction of knowing I was doing a challenging job well.

These thoughts were still floating in my mind when I walked into the meeting, slightly late. As I found a seat on the far edge of the room, I noticed with a smile that Garek Carson was there. He was the director of my portion of the Project, but he'd been away the past two weeks. Suddenly, I realized I was very glad to see him again, though I wasn't really sure why my reaction should be so strong. I'd only known him in a working atmosphere.

Garek, as my section's supervisor, was under tremendous pressure due to the limited time we'd been given to accomplish what turned out to be a huge task. He was a good man for the job because of the wide range of experience he had working with many of Earth's resources. He'd worked not only in the forests division, where Jon and I now worked, but also in other sections that coordinated urban and rural resources on a planetary level. I knew him as a capable manager and supervisor with a good working relationship with people of all kinds.

There were a few times when we hadn't seen eye-to-eye, largely due to my own strong-mindedness. When I saw what I thought was the correct way to do something, I stood up for it, even to someone as high up as Garek.

It said a lot for him that he wasn't offended by my boldness, and when I turned out to be right on some things he acknowledged it.

So my respect for him grew. I could tell his main goal was to do the job right, not just rush through it, even though people from higher up were breathing down his neck. Yet, with all this, he never seemed to lose that broad smile of his. It got to where everyone on the Project recognized his explosive laugh in the hallway, or the way he always took two firm steps into a room, then stopped in silence to survey the situation before he spoke.

We had only one encounter that could be called social rather than professional during the entire Project. It was an evening about two weeks ago when the bulk of the work was finished. I was very tired from long hours, stress, and lack of sleep, and when I saw him sitting alone in the hotel café, I just plopped down next to him because he was a familiar face. He showed no surprise, but just asked how I felt now that the Project was almost done.

Then he began talking excitedly about the prospects of finishing the initial report that night. We shared our thoughts on how the whole thing was going. And yet, with all the pressure on his mind, he had time to listen to my own personal apprehensions about going back to the little office in the tiny rural Valley town. That evening I began to realize what a receptive person he was, to listen to my own little problems when he had so many big ones of his own.

Later that evening, I wrote him a short note, trying to express how good it was to have met him and worked with him.

It was hard to find a right time to give it to him. Finally, as I was taking the last stack of papers to him, at about midnight, I set the colored envelope on top of the pile. "The note is for you," I said, as I handed all the papers to him.

His eyes danced so much I was surprised. I expected him to stuff the note in his jacket, but he ripped open the envelope immediately and read it before it went in his shirt pocket.

"Thank you!" he said, looking straight at me, the intensity in his voice catching me by surprise. Suddenly he embraced me, heedless of who was in the room. I couldn't really sense what he was feeling right then, and I didn't know what I was feeling either.

CHAPTER 11

GAREK

All these memories came back to me in a flood, as I got settled in my seat. I caught Garek's eye as he happened to glance my way, and when he saw me, he broke into his big, crooked smile. It felt like a breath of fresh air in that stuffy room.

When a refreshment break came, I headed straight over to him to say hello. Then as I got closer, I suddenly felt shy and wondered whether to shake his hand or just smile. He solved it for me, by putting a strong arm around my shoulders and giving me a squeeze as we walked through the door into the hallway.

"How's my good friend?" he asked. His voice seemed to glow with joy.

"I'm just fine," I searched for a reply. "I was glad to get here in time for this meeting. Traffic was bad in the city. My supervisor in the Valley didn't think it was important enough for me to come last night."

"Well, I'm glad you were here. You've contributed a lot more to this Resource Project than your supervisor realizes."

"My presentation went well last week," I said, trying not to sound too boastful.

"I'm sorry I was out of town that day. I wish I'd seen it."

Then I found myself asking a question that sounded casual at the time. "Are you commuting from home this week? Or staying here in the city?"

"I'll probably stay up here one more night toward the end of the week."

"Well, maybe we can get together for dinner sometime."

"I'd like that," he smiled.

***

["You know, Martina, this is all feeling very real for me," said Ginna in my head.

"Well, we've never done anything quite like this before," I replied. "Are you doing okay—being 'inside' me, and all?"

"Sure, I'm fine. I just wanted you to know that whatever you feel, I'm feeling, too."

"Just let me know if anything gets to be too much for you."

"Okay."]

Garek and I *[Martina resumed]* both had a lot of work to do the next couple of days, and didn't cross paths. The last day of the work-week, I went to turn in my final summary at the main office. He and a few others were sitting around swapping tales about their experiences in the Forestry Commission. I always enjoyed listening to these stories because it gave me a chance to see how things worked in the agency from an insider view. Gradually, each of the others set out for their homes and evening engagements. I heard myself asking Garek:

"Are you staying in town tonight?"

"Yes," he smiled. "At the Hotel Constellation. How about you?"

"I'm there, too. Would you like to meet for dinner?"

"Sure. I'll stop by your room to pick you up."

"You can just call my room from the lobby." I gave him the room number.

As he wrote it down, he nodded. "I'll call you about 18:30, okay?"

"Sounds fine."

After I left, I wondered if it was traditional for a woman to set a date like that here on Earth. This part of the planet seemed to be more of a backwater of customs than other places I'd lived.

'Well, I'm not from this area,' I thought, 'and I'm just the assertive type, anyway. It doesn't matter. After all,

Garek and I are just friends who both happen to need someone to share a dinner with.'

I admit I felt a warm thrill when I heard his voice on my room transceiver, "Martina, I'm waiting in the lobby."

"Okay. I'll be right down."

Even though I knew he was close to fifteen years my senior, he looked somehow younger when I first saw him standing across the room. Then I realized it was because he had on casual clothes, and I was used to seeing him in his dress uniform. As I came off the lift before he saw me, I just took a moment to gaze at him there, looking strong and handsome.

We went outdoors and walked the city streets for a few minutes, happy to have no stress and no place we needed to be by a certain time. As we strolled past a very ornate and old-looking building, I asked him if he knew what it was.

"Oh, that's the Morotani Temple," he said. "It's stood at the center of this city almost since it was founded eons ago. It's probably the most ancient building still standing in this hemisphere."

I became excited at talk of a temple. "Do they have a fountain in there?"

"I really don't know. I've never been inside. Only the initiated are allowed to set foot in the place. It's a big secret."

I sighed at this. "Ugh! I had enough of secret

knowledge only the faithful can know, on other planets. I'm looking for the True Fountain that washes everyone clean, and I'm told it's free to all who wish to come."

"Wow! I've never heard of that. Where did you hear about it?"

"To make a long story short, we met a hermit while we are traveling in space. He's the one who told us to find Maia—that's what he called Earth. He said the True Fountain would be somewhere on this planet, but we haven't found it yet."

"Well, it's a big planet, and you probably haven't seen a lot of it."

"No, we haven't. It's kind of frustrating."

"Who's 'we'?"

"Oh, yeah—my little brother Jael, and Jon, my—partner."

"Are you married then?"

"Not yet. Where we come from marriage isn't common."

"Oh."

Soon we decided to go into a little cantina, where we glimpsed some fellow-workers through the window. We were seated in another room, however, since the front one was filled already.

We ordered drinks and began to unwind as we waited for our dinners. Once we relaxed, we could talk about almost anything. Our conversation flowed easily from work to families, to recreation we enjoyed, and then career hopes and frustrations. I began to tell him more about myself than I'd told anyone else on the Project.

About halfway through our meal, some Commission people from the Valley Office, which supervised my little rural office, stopped at our table. The Head Manager, Hami Dajah, was among them.

Garek seemed to think it was a good time to tell my top supervisor what a good job I did on the Project. His words pleased me, but I also felt embarrassed to hear him talking about me to the head of all the Valley's operations. I tried to concentrate on my food, but Garek kept talking in such detail I knew I was starting to blush.

When they left, he said, "I hope I didn't embarrass you, but I really meant all that. You were a very important part of the success of this Resource Project. No one could have taken your place or done a better job."

"Thanks, Garek," was all I could manage to say.

"You know, I'm sure your boss will continue to find ways to use your talents. It would be a waste to just put you back to transcribing reports. You wait—things will happen."

This was a very encouraging thought, one I hadn't really dared to consider before. Only a few months ago, I'd been passed over for a job I felt qualified for and really wanted. That left me feeling quite defeated. But hearing him say these things helped to lift my spirits again.

We never seemed to run out of things to talk about. I was enjoying the stimulating conversation so much that I never wanted the evening to end. I ordered another drink, though I knew I shouldn't, just to prolong the meal and our time together. He told me details of his early career, describing all the different places he lived and worked. Since I hadn't seen much of Earth, I was fascinated.

Finally, there was no way around it. It was time to go. Since I was the one who invited him to dinner, I paid my half of the bill. He wouldn't let me pay for his, though.

As I rose from the table, I could tell I'd already drunk too much wine. Before I knew what happened, I almost tripped over a chair. He slipped his arm around me immediately. "Sorry," I laughed lightly. "Guess I can't hold my liquor."

He just smiled.

When we got back to the Constellation, I began to dread the thought of saying good-bye, knowing this would be the last time I'd see him. So I was delighted when he suggested we go to the lounge in the hotel. I knew I didn't need more wine, but I wanted to keep talking to him.

And the conversation continued over another drink. He began to talk about his daughter, a talented musician who wasn't much younger than I. We were both surprised when I told him I played the flute also.

"It seems few people make their own music anymore," I sighed. "My brother Darien played an instrument called a manitar on Terres."

"How many brothers do you have, Martina?"

"Three actually—two older, and one younger. But our oldest brother, Stephen, died while we were still on Terres."

"Oh, I'm sorry. Any sisters?"

"No, I'm the only girl." I was glad when he didn't ask questions about how Stephen died. "Darien and Jael, my remaining brothers, are here on Earth, too. It's so good to be together again."

He smiled and nodded. "Family is pretty important, isn't it? Especially in these turbulent times."

There were a few moments of awkward silence, but then the conversation switched to hobbies, and we found we had many interests in common, like hill-walking and reading books. Even though books were a bit more common on Earth than Terres, it was still unusual to find someone who read them for pleasure.

Then he began to compare our ages, which was no easy task when taking into account the changes caused by my GAP-crossings.

"All it means," I laughed, "Is that you're almost old enough to be my father."

"It's hard to believe that when I was finishing university and starting my career with the Commission, you were only a child."

"Age is only relative, anyway," I shrugged. "It's just a number."

"You haven't mentioned your father," he said then.

I took a deep breath before I replied, "He died in the wars when I was young. And we lost Mother not too long after that—to her grief."

Suddenly he reached across the table and took my hand. "I'm so sorry," he murmured.

"Now you'll probably be analyzing me and thinking I'm just looking for a father-figure, or some psychological thing like that."

I sat there in silence, trying to keep the tears from starting, but my efforts were in vain. Then I felt a movement I couldn't see through my blinded eyes. Next thing I knew, he was sitting beside me on the bench, holding my hand firmly in his.

"What really matters is that two people can communicate with each other," I heard him say.

I took a deep breath and found myself merging into his embrace. "Isn't it interesting how people communicate? Things I can hardly say to anyone, I can say to you, a comparative stranger."

"I know what you mean. But I think it's harder to really communicate with those you're closest to sometimes—like parents and children, or husbands and wives."

"Yes, I have that trouble a lot, with my brothers especially, as much as I love them. I've always blamed myself, feeling I've failed to be a good sister. It was hard on all of us losing our parents so young."

My voice disappeared again and the tears continued to flow.

"Well, I've found that you shouldn't expect too much in any relationship," he said. "Nothing is perfect."

I nodded at this. There were many times I expected too much, especially from Jon. Then I couldn't think of anything else to say. As we sat together there, I began to enjoy the strength and warmth of his touch. His hand seemed so big and strong as our fingers intertwined. I found myself leaning into his shoulder, thinking how solid he felt.

He leaned close and seemed about to kiss me. Instead he breathed into my ear, "You're so soft and warm. My heart seems to have risen right into my throat. I'd like to have a little more privacy with you."

I knew what he meant.

"Can we go up to your room?" he asked.

"Sounds risky." I tried to say that lightly, but my heart was beginning to race. I knew this was the moment when I should smile and say, 'No thanks, it's been a wonderful evening.' But instead I found myself saying, "Sure."

"You know the way, so I'll follow you." His smile was warm, and he gently slipped his arm around my waist until we reached the lobby.

When we stepped into the lift, I wondered if he would try to kiss me there, but he didn't. Not touching each other, we walked down the hall, and it seemed a long way to my door. As we stepped inside, I quickly excused myself to the bathroom. "I've never been good with wine," I smiled.

When I came out, he was standing across the room by the window, but he moved quickly to me, and before I really had time to wonder what it would be like to kiss this man, he wrapped me in a strong embrace, kissing deeply. At that moment, it was a kiss that made me forget all others in my life.

Soon he whispered, "I can't take this much pressure standing up," and he pulled me gently on top of him on the bed.

He kept kissing me and rubbing my back with soft strokes. From somewhere in the deep recesses of my mind, I thought of Father singing me to sleep when I was small. And I felt myself beginning to melt into his warm embrace, feeling loved and safe.

Yet, like a slight haze far behind me somewhere, was the knowledge that I shouldn't be here. This feeling began to battle inside me, trying to push the warm safe feelings out of my mind. I found myself breathless, but finally managed to speak, "You don't give me time to think."

He stopped and smiled into my eyes. "I'll give you all the time you need to think, if that's what you want."

This surprised me. I hadn't met very many patient men. "I just don't know. I mean—I'm with Jon, though we haven't had a formal ceremony. I don't want to hurt anyone."

"I don't want to hurt you," he whispered. "But there's nothing I'd like more than to be right here together, as close as a man and a woman can be."

I nodded, but I couldn't stop the feelings that were rising in my mind all the while.

"I'd do my best to make you happy." He kissed me again. "Let's just make it our evening and not worry about anything else."

I knew I was weakening. His touch was electrifying as he moved his fingers gently down my arms, and then slowly into my tunic.

"Oh, Martina, I just want to make love to you." These last words were almost lost in another breathless kiss. I knew this was the turning point, either stop now, or let go. I let go.

He certainly knew what he was doing, and I wondered where he learned so well how to please a woman. I'd never felt this way with anyone else. At last, we were just lying there together, arms and legs wrapped around each other in quiet reverie.

"I don't want you to leave," I whispered finally.

"Well I don't have to go just yet," he smiled.

"You know, you're very special—like no man I've ever known before."

"You're a very special lady." He smiled that big, crooked smile of his.

We were silent then, and as we lay there together, I enjoyed the fact that he didn't just get up and walk away, once he had his satisfaction. He really *was* like no other man I'd ever met.

We must have slept then, quiet and comfortable in each other's embrace.

Next thing I knew, he was sitting on the edge of the bed, putting on his shoes. Looking toward the window, I could see that the sun was rising.

"I guess you've paid for a room you didn't use," I murmured.

"No matter," he smiled.

Then he stood to go. I moved to the edge of the bed, and he pulled me to him. "Martina, I have strong loving feelings for you. It's been a wonderful evening."

I found myself wanting to reply with equal feeling, but the words stuck in my throat. "Love is an awfully big word," I managed to whisper.

"It's much more than liking," he said.

I stood in silence, resting my hands against his broad chest. I wanted to say something to tell him how I felt for him, but found I couldn't. It just didn't seem right to talk of love to anyone but Jon. I was feeling very confused.

Garek kissed me once more and moved toward the door.

"It's been really beautiful," he said.

"Yes, it has."

He opened the door, and took my hand for an instant. Then he was gone.

I stood there feeling numb. Never had anyone made a good-bye so special. He actually spoke of feelings he had for me, but I found myself looking far back to my dark past that I wanted to forget.

There had been many men, too many. But there hadn't been any sharing of words, thoughts, or feelings—just the gratification of the body. Afterwards, I always had a vague feeling of wanting to be told what all of it meant, or just to know someone cared for me as a person. Besides Jon, Garek was the only one who'd done this, and now I wouldn't have any opportunity to see him again.

What was I supposed to do now?

CHAPTER 12

AFTER-THOUGHTS

The next day I was tired and confused, but my thoughts were also warm and easy as I caressed memories of the night. When I saw him down the hall, our smiles had the same open friendliness as before. I began to realize our friendship started long before last night. In fact, he said something about this somewhere in the night. I remembered the words well:

"It just seemed the right time—everything flowed toward that warm feeling when I took your hand, and then on from there."

I'd never heard a man express himself this way. Here was someone very unique. It almost seemed like some old romantic myth, but this was no legend or tale. It really happened. But if I tried to think about it too much, I wasn't sure what I felt, or where to go from here. I knew I was trying to hide from the part of myself that kept asking, 'What about Jon?'

In the afternoon, he went back to his main office across the city. So I was really surprised when the receptionist came into the meeting I was in and indicated I had a call. As I walked out the door, my heart started pounding, and I was telling myself not to be silly—this couldn't be Garek.

But when I picked up the transceiver earpiece, I could hear his smiling voice right away, "How's it going today?"

"I'm fine."

"That's good." Then he went on to explain that there was a slight discrepancy in the final draft of our report, and he needed me to clarify some data in my section. It made me feel good I could provide the answer for him, and it seemed quite natural to talk business, as we so often did before. When I finished, he surprised me and said, "When you're down here again on some project, as I'm sure you will be sometime, please give me a call. We can go to dinner again."

There was a lot in this statement beyond the words, of course. First, it said he had confidence in my abilities. But mostly it showed he wanted to see me again. I tried to keep my voice calm as I replied, "Sure I will. It would be nice to get together someday."

"We will," he said. "It's a small world."

There was so much more I wanted to say, but no words came. So we just said good-bye.

***

Once I was back home in the Valley, things got a lot harder. My mind was clouded with confusing thoughts and uncertainty. When I came home, I was haunted with how to reconcile my feelings for Garek with my relationship to Jon.

I knew I still loved Jon, and I wasn't sure exactly what it was I felt for Garek, who appealed to me by his empathy and understanding. This was something Jon often lacked, but I knew I was being unreasonable to expect Jon to meet all my needs. Garek met some of those unfulfilled needs, though, and was that so terribly wrong?

Still, I knew I was trying to rationalize, and the truth was I'd given part of my heart to another, feelings I should have kept for Jon alone. But what could I do?

One evening as I watched the sun setting in a red haze, I tried to sort out once and for all what I must do. I told myself to stand by my love for Jon, even if my feelings tried to betray me. Whatever it took, I'd do my best to see this arrangement worked. I hoped somehow things would eventually fall into place, and each relationship in my life would be as it should be.

Finally, my feelings began to subside, like the sun sinking below the horizon. I told myself Garek was just a dear friend, and tried to believe it.

One day, when I'd been back at my old job for about two weeks, I was answering the transceiver and transcribing, like before, when just before lunch, a call came in which I answered.

"Martina?" came a very familiar voice. "Hi, it's Garek."

My heart took a leap. "Well, hi there." I tried to sound as casual as I could.

Most of my co-workers had gone to lunch already, so even though I was at the front desk, it seemed all right to talk to him there.

"I just wanted to talk to you," I heard him saying. "Just to see how you're doing."

"I'm fine," I said. "This is a big surprise to hear from you." Suddenly I couldn't think of anything else to say.

"I've been on vacation since we finished the Resource Project. I really needed it."

So he'd called me as soon as he got back from his vacation. That was interesting. He went on to talk about my work and how he was sure more opportunities would come to me. It felt good to hear him say it, though I didn't have his confidence things would go my way in the Commission.

Suddenly a silence came between us. There was so much I wanted to say, but couldn't on this phone, in this office. Evidently, he had the same problem, for he said casually, "Well the snow season will be here soon."

"Yes. We already have close to a meter on the mountaintops."

"It would be fun to snowshoe sometime," he said.

"I've never tried that, though I'd like to."

"Well, maybe we can someday. I guess I'd better get back to work."

"Yes, I need to eat my lunch. It's the best part of my day here."

He laughed his familiar explosive laugh. "Enjoy it then! We'll be seeing you."

"Yes, I hope. Take care of yourself."

As I hung up the transceiver, I felt a strange numbness. Now all my decisions shifted around me in an emotional earthquake. He was still thinking of me, which seemed to indicate I hadn't been a one-night-stand for him, after all.

This was a totally new experience for me. It filled me with amazement that this man, so much older than I, and in such a high position, saw something attractive in me. He said he felt more than just liking, but I could hardly believe it. I'd always felt somehow unlovable deep down— perhaps because so many men merely used me. Now there were two men in my life who made me feel loved. But what was I supposed to do about it? Anything?

As the rest of the month passed, I forced myself to put Garek into the back of my mind. This couldn't work, I kept telling myself. I needed to be happy with what I had.

CHAPTER 13

CALIEN

"You know, I can really begin to understand how a woman could have an affair with another man."

These words pierced deeply into my very being. My friend Calien had no idea how pertinent her words were, as she said them. I'd gone to see her one evening to catch up on our friendship. Since I'd been gone so much to the city, we hadn't seen much of each other for a long time. She'd become my dearest friend and confidant after we moved to the Valley.

"All it would take," she was saying, "Would be some-one to pay you special attention, praise your talents, really make you feel loved and wanted—or just sweep you off your feet with a kiss. I know myself, there have been times when I'd have gone straight to anyone who showed that kind of interest in *me*."

I smiled and nodded in agreement. Inwardly, I was marveling at how well Calien sensed my situation with

Garek. Did she somehow guess? I didn't think I'd said enough for that. It was uncanny how often she seemed to know just what was troubling me, even before I spoke of it.

Was I that easy to read? And if she could read me like a book, perhaps others—like Jon—could, too. I *had* mentioned Garek to her, and our work in the city, but carefully left out mention of the night we went to dinner, or that he called me here in the Valley. Still, maybe she'd picked up on my feelings, even though I tried to hide them.

Perhaps she was just sharing some of her own experiences, hoping to help me deal with my questions, unspoken or not. At any rate, she was helping me see I wasn't alone in my doubts and feelings—other women had them, too. Calien was also a Believer, and I thought this helped her share these words with me. In fact, she and her partner were actually married.

"Our dear men don't mean to take us for granted," she continued. "It just happens as things fall into the everyday-ness. Know what I mean?"

"Boy, do I! You know, my relationship with Jon is really comfortable. But that means it's not as exciting as it once was. Sometimes I feel like I have to force the emotions to feel stimulated or romantic. It doesn't seem exciting anymore. I guess people just change over time."

"They sure do," she said.

"Calien, I know you've read The Book more than I have. I really want to follow its teaching. What does it say about husbands and wives?"

"Let's take a look," she said, smiling as she took The Book down from its shelf there in her living room. This in itself was a reminder books, and Believers, weren't as rare on Earth as on Terres.

"Here's one verse in the book of *Mark*—we used this at our wedding. The Lord is telling some teachers of the law, 'at the beginning of creation God made them male and female. For this reason, a man will leave his father and mother and be united to his wife, and the two shall become one flesh. So they are no longer two, but one. Therefore, what God has joined together, let man not separate'…" She was only about halfway through this passage when tears began filling my eyes. Somewhere in my chest, I felt like my heart was breaking.

Then a voice in my mind was murmuring between sobs, *'This really is hard for me to hear—what with my parents getting a divorce.'*

'Is that you, Ginna?' I asked in my mind.

'Yes—I'm sorry. It's just I still feel the pain. My father walked out and never looked back. How could he do that to people he used to love?'

'I don't really know, Ginna. My parents stayed together until death parted them. But I still feel the pain of losing them.'

Calien noticed the tears by this time and saw my lips moving. "Are you all right, Martina?" She took my hand in hers.

"I'm not sure. Is this pain just for my dead parents? Or is it my own pain? I've never been the sort of woman the Lord desires. I lost my virginity much too young, and now it's too easy to fall into the arms of any man who makes me feel special."

'It's not just you that does these things,' came Ginna's voice in my head again. 'It's me, too. Wherever you go, I go too, you know.'

"I'm so sorry, Ginna—"

Then I saw Calien looking at me strangely. "Who are you talking to?"

"Uh—it's hard to explain—here, may I please have The Book?"

"Sure," she nodded, as she handed it to me.

My hands rested on the opened pages hesitantly. Then it was as though they were no longer my own. They began turning pages toward the back of The Book, until it fell open to a book called *First Corinthians*.

And then my voice began reading words that I'd never heard before—but I could tell Ginna knew them well:

"Do you not know that he who unites himself with a prostitute is one with her in body? For it is said, 'The two shall become one flesh.' But he who unites himself with the Lord is one with him in spirit. Flee from sexual immorality. All other

sins a man commits are outside his body. Do you not know that your body is the temple of the Holy Spirit, who is in you, whom you have received from God? You are not your own; you were bought at a price. Therefore, honor God with your body."

My cheeks were drenched with tears by the time my voice stopped reading.

Calien handed me a tissue, and I blew my nose loudly. "I'm sorry to be such a mess," I murmured.

She didn't reply but kept a warm hand on my shoulder.

"What can I do now? I've already made so many mistakes. The Lord must hate me."

"How can he hate someone he died for?" she said softly. "There's a story in The Book of a woman who was caught in the act of adultery. The lawyers dragged her to Yeshua—you call him Kristos— and demanded that he put her to death by stoning, which was the penalty back then."

"Ugh! That's bad," I sighed. "So what did he do?"

"The Books says he drew something in the dirt at his feet, then looked up and said, 'Let whichever one of you who has never sinned cast the first stone'."

"And then?"

"One by one, they all walked away, silent and heads down. Then he turned to her and asked, 'Woman where are your accusers?' She looked around and couldn't believe they were all gone. Then she looked at him, as if to ask, 'What should I do now?' And the Lord said to her, 'Go and sin no more'."

"So, he forgave her, and gave her another chance."

Calien nodded. "There are other similar stories in The Book, and I've heard friends tell such stories, too. Just turn it all over to him, the good you've done, along with the bad. He can change it into something beautiful, if you leave it in his hands."

"Thanks, Calien," I sighed.

"Don't thank me, thank God."

Then she held my hands in hers and prayed, "Lord you know that your servant Martina wants to change and do what you want. Please forgive her past, and help her to walk forward with you, into a brighter future."

Somewhere, deep in my mind, I felt a sigh that I knew must be Ginna. 'Thank you,' I breathed to her, too.

Later, as I walked back home in the clear cold of a winter night, I found myself more at peace than I felt for a long while. The icy calm of the night seemed to penetrate me, and I became acutely aware of the pure white softness of the snow, the distant silvery stars. It was always good to visit with Calien. Things seemed to sort themselves out when I talked to her.

***

Sunsets and sunrises flowed by, and weeks passed. Periodic snows continued to fall. Each day, as I walked to work through the cold, white fluff, I felt my thoughts softly drift to Garek, but they were becoming hazier, like a sky full of snow—felt but not really seen clearly.

Then one day, when I was at work, and he was barely in my mind at all, there came a letter. I recognized his scrawly writing as soon as I saw it, for I'd seen his notes on project sheets. Letters were an antique way of sending messages, but this part of Earth was still in a backwater of some of those old ways. It touched me that he'd do something as personal as write out a message himself with his own hand.

My thoughts were suddenly full of him again. When I finally found a spare moment to open the letter unobserved, I read it through quickly. Then, since no one was around, I read it again, more slowly, hanging on each word.

Much of it was conversational, telling what he was working on, wondering what I was doing with myself. But more than that, he again communicated his feelings—so unusual for a man. He said he really valued communicating with me, and I was very special to him.

It was a strange experience seeing those words on paper right before my eyes. It seemed to mean much more when done in this ancient way, in writing. Ever since my childhood, I had a reverence for old ways, something my parents and older brothers taught me.

Here, Garek expressed his feelings for me in a way I already treasured, and this made it all the more meaningful. No one else in my life had ever taken the time to say he really cared like this, except Jon. But at this moment, Jon seemed to pale in the light of this new excitement, this discovery I was special to someone I met only recently.

Then I realized dimly this was exactly what Calien warned of—the danger of new excitement paling the comfortable-ness of the everyday. I could have dealt with Garek treating me only as a sex object, for I was used to that from my past. Oh, I knew Jon loved me for more than just my body. He was the first one who had ever met any of my physical *and* emotional needs.

But now Garek had forged an emotional connection, too, and I was confused, even a little frightened. Was I getting trapped in this tiny town and this dead-end job? I longed to be back in the excitement of the city, and he was getting tangled up in those yearnings. This was not supposed to have happened!

As I walked home that afternoon in the ever-present snow, I found myself talking to Garek as if he were there beside me, "What is it you really want from me? I'm not sure I have enough to give. Right now, there's nothing I can do but be here. Maybe the future will be different, maybe not. There's only now, and this is the place where I have to be."

The words seemed to flow like a song. In fact, I was finding Garek bringing songs out in me, as no one had for a long time. I'd written songs for Jon at the begin-ning, but then they somehow dried up. I knew part of the reason—times when I'd show a song to Jon, and all I'd get was a vague look in his eyes, or a shrug, and words like, "I don't quite see your meaning, Martina." Or, "I guess I'm just not a creative person."

This really hurt and left me needing someone to understand. But now Garek brought these songs out again. I would've liked to sing one of my songs for him, but it was too risky on the transceiver. Perhaps I'd write *him* a letter.

The wind was howling all that week, as it often did here. When it finally stopped, a frigid stillness settled over the Valley, and things began to settle in my mind, too. I wasn't sure if this was a true calm, or just frozen quiet, like the land beyond our windows.

As the winter cold set in, Jon grew colder and more distant, too. I knew I'd caused this myself by the turmoil of feelings I was trying to hide. It was easier to just mentally push him away.

Periodically, I'd be surprised by a call from Garek. He always called me at work, of course. It was obvious neither of us could call from home where someone else might hear us, but I was beginning to get nervous about the calls at work, too. I didn't want to jeopardize his career, or mine.

When he did call, he sounded casual, saying things like he just wondered how I was doing. One time though he said, "Boy, it sure would be good to see you again. Wouldn't it be nice to take a walk on fresh green grass?"

I knew exactly what he meant. The winters were long here in the mountain valleys. And the ache for green grass, fresh air, and spring seemed to affect almost everyone. In spite of knowing better, my thoughts began to fly along bizarre paths after he said this. It would be so good to see him, to go walking together, talk face to face. But of course, this was impossible. How could I hide such a visit from Jon? There was no way. This was just a silly juvenile dream.

So, I tried to calm myself down and forget the whole thing. I forced myself to do my job as it should be done, not pining for something more challenging. I just kept on answering the transceiver and working with the office Terminal, day after day.

Then his second letter came, and the flood gates burst again. He was even more open with his feelings this time. And he sent me a book, one that seemed to express many things he and I felt for each other, and the few wild and open places left here on Earth.

"I hope this book will help you see some of the feelings I have for you," he wrote. "I loved the song you wrote, that you sent in your letter. I wish I could express my feelings as well as you do. Someday, I'd like to try, because there are so many things I want to say."

I was surprised at his candor, and even a bit frightened. Did he mean to say he loved me? How could I ever keep my emotions in check? Or should I just go to him? I was too fearful to risk this, though. I knew Jon loved me, and wouldn't ever let me down. Sure, Garek said he loved me, but was it the kind of love I could stake everything on—and leave Jon? I couldn't even face thinking about it.

Perhaps I'd aroused a response in Garek I wanted subconsciously, but also knew I shouldn't have. It was too late now to un-sing any of the songs I'd sent him. Now I'd just have to wait for another letter or call, to see what happened next. Things were set in motion that I seemingly had no control over anymore.

CHAPTER 14

REVELATION

"Oh, Calien!" I sobbed, "I just feel so tied up inside, like everything is a terrible confusion, a whirling storm."

Calien, in her tenderhearted and understanding way, embraced me. "Martina, my dear friend, I wish I could do something for you. Just have faith—please don't lose that. I'm praying for you."

"I used to pray," I sighed. "But ever since my oldest brother Stephen died, I think I've forgotten how. It's like the Lord isn't listening anymore. Back then I just wandered off to do what I thought would make me feel better. You don't want to know how many terrible things I've done."

She kept holding my hand. All I could do was hang onto her, speechless, with tears streaming down my cheeks. Such a dear friend—and seemingly the only thing I had left to cling to. Once the tears subsided, I tried to find words to express what was in my heart, "How can I ever find my way back to the Lord? Why can't I just be free to do what feels right?"

"Martina, the Lord isn't trying to make us unhappy with lots of rules. He wants to give us true joy, not the fleeting happiness that just comes and goes, like mists on the mountains."

"Where I grew up, the Council and the System gave us long lists of rules we were supposed to follow, but I ran away from that."

"And did it help?"

"Not really. I fell into a deeper, darker pit than I was in before. For awhile I lost all sense of who I really was. I didn't even remember my own little brother, Jael."

"So just doing what felt good didn't work, did it?"

"No, I guess not. But isn't it my own tendency to be hard on myself that won't let me stay happy?"

"Well, I don't know about that. But perhaps it's the Lord trying to say, 'I want something better for you than this. Please trust me'."

"Calien, I know there's no one in the world who means more to me than Jon. He and I have been through so much. I never thought I'd feel worthy of marrying any-one, but I'm wondering now. I know he loves me, but I keep seeing ways he can't meet all my needs. So I don't know what to do."

"No single person can meet all of another's needs, Martina."

"I know. But I've found someone else who meets needs Jon can't."

I realized even as I spoke those words this was my greatest need right now, to get some of this out in the open with someone else.

"Who is it?" she asked.

"Garek Carson."

"Wasn't he your supervisor, when you were working on that project in the city?"

"Yes, he was. Do you think it's wrong to have a friend who's a man?"

"No, it's not wrong. But you do have to be careful. It depends on what you mean by 'friend'."

"We write some letters back and forth." I knew I was trying to make it sound innocent, but Calien was very perceptive.

"Well, just by the way you're talking, it sounds to me like he's an intimate friend. You really have to be careful, Martina, if you start comparing him to Jon, or expect Jon to be like him."

"I know." How was it Calien always seemed to see through my words to the truth? Was I that transparent with everyone? This was a very frightening thought, so I tried to change the subject.

"Do you ever feel the mountaintop experiences The Book tells about, Calien?"

"Sometimes I do—when I feel like everything is wonderful, and even like a little bit of Heaven."

"But it never lasts," I moaned.

"Well, when Kristos took three of his followers to a mountaintop to show them his glory, they wanted to build shelters and stay."

"But they had to go back down to the valley."

"Yes, and here we are in this Valley, as we call it. You know, Martina, the valleys are where the work gets done, where the farms are, and the crops grow, and where the people live. Up in the mountains, it's only wild land, around here, at least."

"They do cut trees for timber up there," I said.

"But they have to bring it down to the Valley to make something useful from it."

"Okay, I get the point. We can't live on the mountaintop. We can only visit it, experience it, and then come back down to the valley."

She nodded. "And live in the everyday-ness."

***

Soon after this, a long letter arrived from Garek. I'd never known a man who wanted to express his feelings this much. It was almost unbelievable, and it swept me off my feet again.

"Martina," he wrote, "I don't know where this is all going to lead, but I feel I must be open with you. I really do love you, and I would like to spend more time with you and get to know you better. I can understand your hesitation, since you hardly know me. And we both recognize the risks we'd be taking. But I only want to see you happy. I don't want to hurt you, or make promises I can't keep."

This said a lot, but I wasn't sure what to think. What did he mean in that last sentence about promises he couldn't keep? Was he saying he couldn't give me any long-term assurances? So how could I decide what to do next?

My past attempts at love had been a series of disasters, perhaps for the same reason. I got emotionally involved with people who were only seeking the physical, while I was building castles of dreams in the air, only to have them come crashing down. Reality was never up to my hopes and dreams. Each time I thought I was in love, it turned out to be only physical. No special meaning, no ideals, no air-castles.

Jon was the only one who was different. The castle we built hadn't been in the air, but on solid ground. Now, though, even *that* castle was beginning to crumble a bit at the corners. Still, perhaps there was a way I could repair it, if only I could keep my own feet on the ground.

***

The winter seemed to be pressing in around me. Some of the locals called this "cabin fever." Snow just kept falling, a little more each day, as if the world would never be anything but white, ever again.

Sometimes I felt like screaming inside or running away. I didn't hear from Garek for several days, then weeks, and began to think my suspicions were right. This, too, was just another castle in the air.

I couldn't help dropping hints of my discontent—complaining and acting depressed. Even when I knew I shouldn't carry on this way, I just couldn't help myself. It was like a groundcar careening down a steep hill. A certain point was reached where stopping was not an option anymore.

Perhaps I didn't realize how much Jon was reading into my emotional state, until the evening we came crashing together like two asteroids on a collision course.

I was saying what I often did, as we finished supper dishes, "I can't take this backwater town anymore. I have to go to the city—get out of this valley of snow."

Jon suddenly threw a dish down into the sink. I'd never seen him get this angry. "I've had it with you and your whining! Why can't you just grow up and act like an adult?"

"I know I'm being too demanding," I sobbed. "But I have needs and feelings, and I just need you to understand."

"I'm sick and tired of trying to understand you, Martina! That's all you ever say, 'understand me!' I can see you want to leave. Why don't you just pack up and go tomorrow—or now, for that matter?"

Now I knew I'd made some terrible mistake, pushing

him too far. There was no turning back now, and this really scared me. I tried to find words to calm him down.

"Jon please, you're over-reacting. I'm getting that cabin fever—just feeling down."

But he suddenly exploded from the chair he'd moved to, and began throwing pillows all over the room. "I'm sick and tired of going over and over the same old things with you!"

I tried to keep my voice calm when I replied this time. "Maybe we just haven't resolved it yet. I can't help that."

"What do you want me to say?" He kept on shouting and throwing things, as though I hadn't even spoken. "Should I say, 'I hate you!' Is that what you want to hear?"

I was going into shock. Why was he saying such things? How had I caused this? It seemed too late for any words now. I felt myself getting numb. Was this what it was like? To end it all, so suddenly? Slowly I began putting on my boots. Perhaps if I left and gave him time to cool off.

"What are you doing?" he demanded.

"I think I'd better just go," I murmured.

He didn't say a word then. I didn't have time to think about what to take, except for my warmest coat, my keys to the groundcar, and whatever credits I had in my wallet. I walked out into the cold winter night and closed the door behind me.

***

For the first hour or so, I just drove south and gave no thought to where I was going. All I knew was that the only road out of the Valley went south. If I kept going for a couple more hours, I'd be in Salien, where Garek was. But what then? I had no idea where his home was. I wasn't even sure of the location of his office.

'I must be crazy to be doing this.' I told myself. Snowflakes were beginning to fill the air, reflecting back the beams of my car's headlights. I could barely see where the edges of the road were. This was not good.

After another hour of very slow driving, I came to the junction with the western road leading to Celeton. Without thinking, I found myself turning that way, instead of continuing on the road to Salien. Perhaps my numb mind knew subconsciously that what I really needed right then was family. So, I drove on toward the city where Darien and Jael lived.

The snow began to let up, shortly after I turned west. I was able to pick up my driving pace, hoping to be in Celeton before Darien got up for work. My mind, for once, was numb. I wasn't feeling anything for anyone—not Jon, not Garek, no one.

All I knew was Jon said he hated me—Jon who was my only haven in the storms. I never meant to hurt him. But sometimes it seems we hurt those we love the most. Maybe that's why Garek was afraid of hurting me. But I didn't really feel anything for him right then. I just kept on driving.

The sun was peeking out of clouds behind me as I reached the outskirts of Celeton. It was a larger city than Salien, but I knew my way around here, since I'd brought Jael here the past two winters to be with Darien.

And so, as the sun began to send light across the tops of the apartment buildings, I pulled up in front of Darien's flat. There were no lights in his window, and I hoped this meant they were still in bed.

Darien had given me a key, so I let myself in as quietly as I could. The flat was still, but I could hear someone softly snoring. Good, they were still asleep. I slipped into the kitchen and made myself a cup of moffee. This was something I still liked of our past from Terres. It was sweeter and creamier than the coffee most people on Earth preferred. I never asked Darien how he managed to get it, for I knew he had connections all over the Galaxy, through his Rebel friends.

The smell must have awakened him, as I secretly hoped it would. When he stepped into the kitchen, his eyes seemed to pop open when he saw me.

"Martina! What are you—?"

"Want a cup?"

"Uh, sure."

I didn't like the heavy feeling of silence in the room, so I babbled as I made the second cup, "I remember how I made Jael get me a cup of moffee the morning you left for the Inland Raiders. I was hung over from—well anyway, I needed moffee, if I was going to function. Poor Jael had never made it before, but he wanted desperately to see you off, so he managed."

"And I did glimpse you as I was boarding."

He took the steaming cup and sipped gingerly, so as not to burn his tongue.

We both sat down, facing each other over the cups as we set them on the table. Silence loomed again, but this time I could think of nothing to say.

"What are you doing here, Martina?" he finally asked.

"Can't a girl come visit her brothers once in a while?"

"Well, of course you're always welcome. But this isn't like you, to drop in so early and unannounced."

"I—uh, Jon and I had a fight."

"I wondered."

"He got so angry I was afraid. No matter what I said, he kept throwing things."

"That doesn't sound like Jon at all."

"I know. Anyway, I just started driving, and ended up here. I thought about going to Salien, but-"

"All right, who's in Salien? Come on, Sis, you can tell me."

The words were dying in my chest, though. Tears were starting to come, and there was no way to stop them. He reached across the table and took my hands in his.

"I can see you're hurting, but I don't know why," he whispered.

"I'm just so confused," I managed to say.

We sat for a long time in silence. Darien kept holding my hands, and then reached up and tried to wipe away some of the tears.

"Jon said he hated me," I murmured.

"What have you done?"

"Me? I'm just so tired of living in that little backwater town, and the winters there seem to never end."

"And-"

"I met someone when I was working in Salien. He's been calling and writing me. I—uh, we had sort of an affair the last time I was there."

"I see—just sort of?" He was smiling slightly.

"Okay—a tryst, I guess you'd call it. I slept with him only once. There are some things about him that I really do love, like how he understands me and values my talents, especially the work I did for him there on the Resource Project. Sometimes I just want to see him again so badly."

"Why did you come here, instead of going to him?"

"We only talk at work. I don't know how to find him."

"Ah—let me guess. This man is in his forties, in Earth years."

"How did you know?"

"Well, it's what some people call 'The Midlife Crisis'."

"The what?"

"It's something that happens to some men when they reach those middle years. They want to try to recapture their youth. And often they take up with a younger woman. The danger and excitement of an affair makes them feel young again."

I felt angry and hurt, all at the same time. "Garek doesn't want to just use me like that. He really cares. You should see what he writes in his letters."

"Are you saving those letters?"

I nodded.

"Perhaps Jon has seen one?"

"I don't think so. Maybe *I'm* just too easy to read—like a book."

"You do wear your heart on your sleeve, Martina." He paused for almost a full minute, then went on, "So what happens now?"

"I have no idea."

We sat in silence for a long time. Darien got up and made us two more cups of moffee. When he returned, his dark green eyes bored into me as he looked across the table. The words he spoke next seemed to come out of nowhere, and yet as soon as he said them, I wondered if the Lord was using him to tell me what I needed to hear, not what I wanted to hear:

"Submitting is such a difficult thing for us humans," he said. "It goes against our very nature to put ourselves under anyone or anything. We want to be special, to be noticed, to be first—every one of us. And yet The Book tells us, 'Submit to one another out of reverence for Kristos.' Then it reminds wives to submit to their husbands."

"Why should The Book pick on women like that?"

"Perhaps this is an area more women seem to have trouble with," he shrugged. "But it gets on men's case too."

"How?"

"It tells husbands to *love* their wives, with the kind of love God has for all of us—the kind of love that sacrifices everything."

"But Darien, Jon and I aren't married yet."

"Perhaps you should be. I know Jon wants to marry you. How do you feel about it?"

"I don't know. I guess I'm being selfish and do have a problem with submission. I want to be my own boss. But I also want someone to tell me how much he loves me." Then it hit me, "That must be why I'm so vulnerable to Garek, who expresses feelings better than most men."

"Sometimes Jon has a problem expressing his emotions," he added.

"And yet I know he really loves me. But now I've broken a tie—or burned a bridge. Maybe it's too late."

More tears were streaming down my face by now.

"Do you still love Jon?"

"Of course!"

"Then you need to focus on that and turn away from temptation."

"I wish Garek and I could still be friends," I sighed, finally wiping tears with the tissue he offered.

"That could be a delicate balancing act and maybe too risky, Sis."

I tried to nod, but ended up dropping my head onto my crossed arms on the table. Suddenly, I realized how weary I was. I'd driven all night, after all.

"Martina, you have so much talent and potential. I just know the Lord is going to use you in a special way, if you'll really submit to him."

Not long ago, I wouldn't have listened to any of this. Part of me was still rebelling against these ideas, the part that wondered why I hadn't gone to find Garek instead of coming here.

'Somehow, I would've found his office,' I thought. 'Surely he wouldn't have left me out on the street. But what if he was out of town?'

"I'm really glad you came to me, Martina." Darien said softly.

"Well, family seemed like the right way to turn."

Just then we heard a surprised noise, and before I could say a word, Jael jumped into my arms.

"Martina! What are you doing here?"

I hugged him tightly. "I wanted to see you and Darien," I said into his hair. "You look like you've grown another few centimeters."

He quickly stood and pulled up to his full height,

"You think so?"

"You bet!"

"How long are you staying?"

I glanced at Darien, wondering what to say.

"Maybe a couple of days, Squirt," he said. "Now you need to get dressed for school."

"Oh, all right. I just hope you'll still be here when I get home."

He trailed off toward his room. But I could see that his feier-cat stayed with us.

"How is he doing?" I asked quietly.

"He's fine," said Darien, "And doing very well in school."

'Jael is blooming here,' said Feier in my mind. 'We're both happy, but we do miss you and Jon.'

I was glad Feier didn't ask me how Jon was doing. While the feier-cat and I were communicating, Darien went into his room and changed into day clothes. Just as he came back into the galley, the transceiver let out a tone.

My heart dropped into my stomach, 'Maybe it's Jon,' was my first thought.

It was. I could tell, just from Darien's end of the conversation, "Yes, she's here… No, she's fine… Yes, we'll be home this afternoon… All right, see you then."

"So, I guess he's coming to collect me," I muttered.

"More like he's coming to tell you how much he loves you."

I wasn't sure I was ready to hear that. I'd felt too many strong emotions in the past few months. Somehow, I thought I might explode if any more emotions got stuffed into my heart.

"Darien?"

"Yes?"

"Are you busy this morning?"

"No. Why?"

"I would really like to take a walk with you, on ground that isn't covered with snow."

"I think I can manage that," he smiled. "Let's get some breakfast, and I'll get Jael off to school."

The weather in Celeton was much warmer than in the Valley. It felt so good to walk in the morning sunshine, watching water-birds on the pond in the city park, and finding places where tiny flowers were beginning to peek up through the grass.

"Spring really is going to come—here at least," I sighed.

"Oh, it will come to the Valley, too."

"Eventually," I chuckled slightly.

"Do that again."

"What?"

"Laugh. You have such a nice soft laugh."

This talk about laughter was reminding me of Garek and his strange explosive laugh. I didn't want think of him, so I grabbed some dead grass from a pile beside the walkway and threw it into Darien's hair. He responded by doing the same. Soon we were chasing each other all over the park, laughing and throwing grass, until we finally collapsed into a heap.

When I caught my breath, I turned to him. "Darien, thank you."

"For what?"

"For being you. I love you, big brother."

He was silent for a long time, looking down at the grass and pulling at it with his fingers.

"That really means a lot, Sis," he said at last. "I know I can never be like Stephen was to you."

"And you're not supposed to be," I said quickly. "You're you. Each of my brothers is special. I always loved when you'd get out your manitar and sing to me—or let me play my flute with you. You have unique talents, you know. And now that you're following the True Lord, I see you as sort of—well, my rock. I guess that's why I came here last night."

"Boy, I sure hope I can live up to all that."

"But what should I do now?" Before I realized it, the tears had started again.

"Do you love this Garek?"

"I don't know for sure."

"And do you still love Jon?"

"Yes, but I don't know if he loves me anymore."

"He's driving all this way to come see you."

"But what do I say to him?"

"Just wait and see what you feel when he gets here. Follow your heart, Sis."

***

We finished lunch and washed up by the time Jon arrived. I heard him speaking to Darien in the hallway, after he answered the knock on the door. My heart started to race.

When the two of them walked into the living room, I could see Jon's face was pale and his eyes were red. Had he really been crying? Or was it just lack of sleep?

"Martina," his voice came softly. "I'm so sorry. Please forgive me."

Now I felt even worse, because I knew I was the one who should be begging forgiveness. Instead, I just stood and wondered what to do. Then he reached a hand toward me, and silently moved us to a cushion in the corner. I saw Darien discretely move off into his bedroom.

As Jon placed his hands over mine and began to pray softly, tears returned to my cheeks. My body was full of pain suddenly, but it was flowing out of me with the tears. I tried to concentrate on his words, but they were a blur. Still, a feeling of cool relief came over me. Slowly I began to hear some of his words:

"Lord, help us to trust you…help us to see what plan you have for us…since you brought us together."

'Yes,' I thought. 'I've been too busy trying to make my own plans.'

When Jon's voice stopped, I tried to find words of my own. "Lord, I'm sorry—help me—help us be more understanding. And, Lord, please help me get back to where I was with you long ago before Stephen died."

Jon drew me into a hug as I said this and whispered into my hair, "I can never be Stephen for you, Martina."

I nodded wordlessly.

"But I want to be the best man I can. Will you let me try?"

"Of course I will. No one has ever treated me as well as you have, except my family."

"We could become a family, you know," he murmured.

I nodded again but wasn't sure what else to say. Yes, he was committed to me, but I knew I was totally unworthy.

CHAPTER 15

GOD'S SENSE OF HUMOR

I went back to the Valley with Jon the next day, after we'd enjoyed a quiet evening, visiting with Darien and Jael. It seemed Jon and Darien were beginning to come to terms with each other, and it was such a relief to me not to feel caught between them, for a change.

I truly wanted to put Garek totally out of my mind. But then something happened I'd wanted all winter. Only now was not the right time—I began to wonder if the Lord had any sense of timing—or was it a quirky sense of humor?

Garek called my office while I was gone. When I went back to work, there was a message to contact him. With my hands trying not to shake, I put in the number he left. His assistant answered, and I asked to speak to him, but didn't give my name. "Hello?" came the voice I knew too well.

"This is Martina."

"Martina?" I could hear the joy in his voice. "Where have you been?

"I-uh—went to visit my brothers in Celeton."

"How are they doing?"

"Just fine."

"How are you doing?" I could hear the tone of his voice change to less of the casual air he had started with.

"Oh—I've had a bad case of cabin fever."

"Winter is tough sometimes, isn't it?"

"Yeah, especially in these remote mountain valleys."

"Martina, the reason I really called is to find out if you could help me with a presentation. There's a conference that wants to use our project as an example. Do you think your boss would let you come?"

'Come?' I thought. 'Now—of all times—*now* I get to see him?' Still, I couldn't resist being part of some significant work again. "I can ask him," I heard myself saying. "Where is this conference?"

"It's down here in Salien."

"You know, maybe it would work better if *you* asked my boss."

"Actually, I already did, when I couldn't get hold of you."

'What?' I thought in panic. 'It looks like I have no choice.'

"Well?" his voice asked over the transceiver. "Did I overstep myself?"

"Uh—no, I guess I'm okay," I said, despite parts of my brain that were saying otherwise.

And so, it was arranged, just as spring finally came to the Valley. The snow was still crusted to the ground, and mornings were chill, but slowly the piles of snow melted and settled, pulling away from the houses and streets. There was still a lot of white to be seen when I looked out my window, but the sun shone almost every day. What a relief that was!

I told Jon my supervisor from last year's project needed me to help with a presentation, which was all true. I made sure he knew this hadn't been my idea. He didn't say anything one way or the other, but saw me off at the air shuttle terminal.

When I arrived at the Salien shuttle terminal, Garek was there to meet me. Before I could say or do anything, he had me in a big, warm embrace. I could see the smile dancing in his eyes—they were so very expressive.

Driving into town in his groundcar, I tried to make casual conversation about what books we were reading, where things were now with the project, whether I had any job prospects.

When we reached the lodge where the conference was to be held, he pulled the groundcar into an underground parking garage. He took my bag from the back of the car, and carried it for me. As we came around a pillar near the door, he suddenly pulled me to him, and kissed me hard.

"I've wanted to do that for so long," he sighed.

I found myself kissing him back—I'd wanted this for a long time, too.

Once we got into the lodge, we acted like casual colleagues. He had many co-workers here and didn't want to make any waves. In a way, it was a relief for me. I wasn't sure how long I could hold out with his kisses.

The first day of the session was exciting for me, getting back into the swing of public relations, the work I really wanted to be doing. I felt at home in front of the audience, giving my part of the first presentation. Then I sat back to watch Garek do his portion. I found myself falling into memories—the excitement, as well as the pressure, of the project—the friends made.

During the morning break, I visited with some of these friends I hadn't seen for several months. Garek hung in the background.

When the afternoon sessions ended, we made our escape—meeting at the lodge parking garage to go for an evening walk in the nearby hills. I could sense he felt we'd be safe from any prying eyes out on the forest trails.

There was still a little snow in the woods under the trees, but not enough to prevent easy hiking. The late evening sun lingered, as the days lengthened with spring's coming. I found myself talking about my family and my visit with my brothers.

"We were always very close as a family," I said. "Often, we did things together—played games and such. We were mostly isolated on Terres because of our religious beliefs."

"Really?"

"Yes. We didn't believe in the System and all it stood for. Our father taught us to worship and serve the True Lord."

"Hmm. I haven't really learned much about the System," he said. "Here on Earth, we've probably kept a lot of the older ways."

"Yes, you have," I said. "In fact, I think Father would've wanted us to come back here to Earth, if it had been possible."

"Why didn't you?"

"Well, you wouldn't believe how hard it is to find this place. The System has erased it from all the maps, databases—everything."

"Why?"

"I guess it has something to do with not wanting to undermine the power they have over people's minds."

"Gosh, I feel like I've lived a very sheltered life here. How did you find Earth—finally?"

"My brother Darien joined the Rebels," I whispered. Even here I worried about listening ears. "They knew where Maia—or Earth—was."

"It's hard for me to imagine all you've experienced. I've never even been in space."

"Well, our experiences were exciting, but some of it was very hard."

We found a dry rock and sat in silence for a long time then, watching the sunset.

"You know something?" he whispered.

"What?"

"I really love you, Martina."

A big lump came into my throat. "I have a lot of feelings for you, too," I managed. "But I'm not sure what I should do with them."

"What do you mean?"

"Well, my friend Calien and I have been reading in The Book about what God intends marriage to be, and I have a lot to learn."

"Um, I think I see what you're getting at."

"And when I was in Celeton, my brother Darien and I had a long talk. I didn't tell you the whole story about that—I went there because Jon and I had a fight."

This time, he didn't speak at first, but just took my hand in his. "So how are things with Jon, now?" he finally asked.

"We made up, and it's so ironic that once he and I sorted things out, this call came from you."

"You could have turned me down, you know."

"And, to be honest, I'm not really sure why I didn't. But you'd already talked to my supervisor and it didn't seem professional to back out like that."

"Well, I'm glad you didn't."

Then I found I was at a loss for words. So, we sat there, watching the rays of light lengthening across the snow-patched ground. I needed to change the subject, so I started talking about the Valley:

"You should come to see it sometime, Garek. The Modox Mountains are truly spectacular. There are lots of places to hike, and rivers to paddle on."

"Yes, I'd like that," he said. "I'd probably bring my family."

"That would be nice. I'd like to meet them someday."

"Well, I do think my children are pretty neat—my daughter plays the flute really well."

"I played the flute when we lived on Terres. I wonder if Earth flutes are the same."

"Yeah, me too. It would be interesting to compare. My son is younger. He's in a 'growing pains' stage, sort of awkward, like a young colt, but I know he'll turn out fine."

"You sound just like a father."

"Do you want to have children, Martina?"

"I guess I hope to someday."

We lapsed into silence again, and I was thinking of how he never mentioned his wife—only his children. I snuggled up against his warm body. With the sunset, it was getting chilly.

Soon we made our way back to the car, still hand-in-hand. No one was around to see us when we re-entered the lodge and made our way up to his room.

It seemed no effort at all for him to pull me gently on top of him on the bed.

"I'm not used to love affairs like this," I murmured. "I suppose this is nothing new for you."

"I had a couple of affairs, but they were just fun and games."

"I'm not a fun and games type of person."

"No," he breathed in my ear. "You're a very deep person."

"I guess I am. It's not easy, though. I tend to expect others to be deep, too. And usually they're not, so I get hurt."

"Have there been many heartbreaks?" he asked, rubbing my back gently.

I didn't want to talk about my past, so I shrugged. "No more than the average, I guess."

He drew me closer again and whispered into my ear, "I want to make love to you again, but I'm almost afraid to ask."

"I'm afraid, too."

"Of me?"

"No. More of myself. Of whether I'll be able to handle it later—or face Jon—who I'm supposed to marry."

"Martina, I love you. Please just stay with me this one more time. I promise not to hurt you—ever."

Tears were beginning to form in the corners of my eyes. "I'm sorry, Garek. Part of me wants to be with you, but part of me knows I need to stay with Jon."

He rolled onto his side, pulled me close, and snuggled my back against his chest. As he kept holding me, I felt safe and warm, almost like I was a child. Maybe what I was looking for all this time *was* a father-figure. But after only a few moments, I sat up, moving a little away from him.

"It is amazing, Garek, the patience you have with me."

"What do you mean?"

"Just to stay here, not angry that I won't sleep with you."

"Maybe I just haven't given up hope that you'll give in," he chuckled.

I stood up then, and moved to a chair beside the desk. I'm not sure why I asked the next question. "Garek?"

"Yes?"

"What do you think about God?"

"What do I think about God? Well, I guess he's important to some people—like he was to your family."

"Yes. My parents said they wanted us to know the truth, so we could judge for ourselves. They died because of their beliefs—the System finally took them from us, in one way or another. My father died in the war, and Mother—well we don't know for sure—they just took her away, for 'rehabilitation', they said—and we never learned what happened to her."

I was trying to keep the tears back as I spoke, but I guess he could hear them. "I'm so sorry. Martina."

"My oldest brother, too—Stephen—he died in a shut-tle crash, but the circumstances were strange. Then Darien had to leave to earn a living for us. Jael and I were left alone. When things seemed like nothing would ever save us, Jon came along, and somehow the Lord used him to help us."

"Now I see why Jon is so special to you."

"Actually, you don't know the half of it."

"Maybe," he whispered.

"I can't talk about it anymore right now."

"So, you want to know what *I* think about God," he said then. "Well, right now I'm wondering why he put you and your family through so much."

"I've wondered that a lot. Now I see how each of them, in their own way, gave their life for what they believed. And now it's up to the rest of us to keep their sacrifice from being in vain."

"That's a really big responsibility to take on—when you're so young."

"Well, we didn't really have any choice."

"But you *have* chosen to stay true to this Lord your parents taught you about."

"Well, there's a passage in The Book which says, 'If the world hates you, keep in mind that it hated me first.' This tells me we shouldn't be surprised when we're persecuted for our faith. Anyway, I haven't done such a good job of being faithful."

"Who's talking in that passage you just quoted?"

"Kristos, the True King. He's also been called Yeshua, here on Earth."

"And what's 'The Book'?"

"People on Earth called it The Bible, which means the same thing in some ancient language. It tells what God is really like, and his plans for us."

"Please tell me more about this."

I was very glad to hear him say this. He seemed to really want to talk now. "Well," I went on, "I believe the Lord loves us, and has a special plan for each of us. Not that we're puppets on a string, just the opposite. We have the choice to listen to him or not."

"You're not a fatalist, then?"

"No, and not a Nosticene or a Colassene."

"A what?"

"Oh yeah, you haven't been in space. They were on this planet, Platius. One side said no one was allowed any pleasure, and the other said anything goes."

"I think I'd lean more toward the second one," he chuckled.

"But those Colassenes were really scary. They had air-drugs that got everyone high, whether they wanted to or not. No one could even remember what they did during their orgies."

"Well, maybe I wouldn't have liked it, after all. I like remembering how happy you've made me."

"Anyway, I believe that what I do matters. But the

problem is I'm only human and can never be good enough to be perfect, like the Lord would like."

"Well, all we can do is try our best, and hope the good somehow outweighs the bad in the end. Right?"

"But what if even our very best still isn't good enough?" I asked.

There was silence for a while, both of lost in our own thoughts.

"You know," he said at last, "I've heard of this Yeshua, and I think he was a special person—who tried to teach us about God."

"I haven't heard that name for him except in The Book. Most people just say 'Kristos' where I come from, if they mention him at all. I guess it's because you're still here on Earth, where people remember his first coming."

"I think he taught us a lot about how to be good."

"He did more than that, though. I believe he bridged the gap between us and God. The Book says he paid for our sins when he died. He did for us what we couldn't do for ourselves."

Garek didn't reply to this, and silence settled around us again.

Finally, he spoke. "You know, I've never felt this comfortable talking about religion with anyone before."

I breathed a sigh of relief. "I'm glad. Some people get really nervous."

"Oh, I'm very relaxed," he smiled, and reached for my hand.

I moved slightly toward him and looked into his eyes. "I wonder if I'll ever see you again," I murmured.

"It's hard to say, Martina."

I felt my heart sinking. I couldn't bear to think of his disappearing from my life entirely, but deep inside I knew it was for the best.

"I know you have to leave early tomorrow," I said at last.

"I wish I didn't."

"I think I should go, so I won't be in your way in the morning."

"You could never be in the way."

"But I know it's time for me to leave," I sighed.

I sat up, and pulled myself together. As he walked me to the door, he gave me one more long, lingering kiss. I motioned him to stay in his room, so I could go down the hall alone. As I started to turn away, he held my arm for a moment more, and looked deeply into my eyes, as though he was trying to memorize my face—or perhaps communicate something silently. But finally, I had to pull away.

"I do love you, Garek—in my way." I whispered. "But I'm afraid this is good-bye."

"I know," he smiled.

That was the last time I saw Garek. I felt sad, but also relieved. After all the turmoil my emotions had put me through, the everyday-ness—as Calien called it—was a peaceful break in the pattern of my life.

***

One night a couple of weeks later, I sat at our small table with pen and paper, knowing I had to get this over with. But how to put all this into words? Now I can't remember all I wrote, but some of it stands out in my mind:

Dear Garek,

First off, please don't think I'm judging you or saying I'm a better person than you are. Far from it. Yes, I profess to be a Believer in the True King, as my family taught me. But I'm a very inconsistent one, and I've made a lot of mistakes over the years.

Yet I want to change, so although part of me wants to be with you, another part knows I belong with Jon. The King brought us together in strange circumstances I can't even begin to describe. I owe Jon my life, and I know he's committed to me. I need to try to live up to that, even though I've done a poor job so far.

I told you a little about my parents and oldest brother, who gave their lives for what they believed. Now it's up to me and my two remaining brothers to carry on. Up to now, I've done a terrible job, but I hope it's not too late to change—for the King to somehow change me.

This is something I've never been able to do before, to turn away from someone who says he loves me. But I know I must, or someday I'll regret it. Maybe I'm developing a conscience, something I probably never had before.

I can't bear to think of you disappearing from my life forever, but something deep inside says this must be. So, this has to be 'good-bye'—God be with you.

Martina

CHAPTER 16

A CHILD'S EYES

As the next few days passed, I tried to focus on the everyday-ness, as Calien called it, hoping this would help me find some peace. A few weeks later, though, I was still weepy and moody. Then one morning I began the day leaning over the toilet, throwing up.

'Perhaps I've caught a virus,' I told myself.

Jon was working in the spring logging camp now. Most of the slush and mud of what the locals called "Spring Breakup" was finally drying out. Once again, the equipment used to fell and haul in trees could get off the roads without sinking up to the axles.

As the afternoon wore on, I didn't seem to be able to get up the energy to move out of our one large comfortable chair. 'I guess I *am* really sick,' I thought. By the time Jon came home, I'd been lying there dozing for almost the whole day.

When he walked in the door of our little cabin, I jerked awake.

"What's for supper?" he asked, looking at me curiously.

"I feel awful," I shrugged. "Even the thought of food makes me queasy."

He dropped down onto the only other seat we had, a low bench beside our kitchen table. "I'm starved," he sighed.

"Okay, I'll see what we have left over from yesterday."

But soon after I got up and tried to get something out of the cooler, I was back in the toilet—throwing up again.

Jon came over to me and patted me gently on the back. "I'm sorry. You really are sick, aren't you?"

"I can't figure it out," I shrugged.

"You just lie back down, and I'll find something for myself."

"Could you maybe just get me some of those white crackers?"

The next day was nearly the same, and the next few after that. I never seemed to get sicker, and I didn't feel better, unless I nibbled on some crackers.

One day I found myself bursting into tears for no apparent reason. In the evening Jon found me that way, sitting at the kitchen table, when he came home.

"What's the matter?" He quickly came and gave me a hug. "Are you sick again?"

"I feel sick a lot lately," I moaned.

He just sat there beside me for a long time. Then he took my hand and rubbed his thumb across the palm, in a way he often did. It was a gesture I found very comforting, most of the time. Today, though, nothing seemed to stop the tears.

"Say, Martina?"

"Hmm?"

"When was your last period?"

"My period?"

He nodded silently.

I hadn't even thought about this. "Let me think—about seven or eight weeks—oh!"

He was smiling into my eyes.

"Good grief!" I suddenly realized I'd never been this late before.

"It looks like we're pregnant," he grinned.

"Well, I guess it could be that. But it's too soon to tell for sure."

"I spent enough time with the Redlarks to know the signs, Martina."

I just stared into his eyes. "So you think you're an expert on this?"

"Well, I did have a couple of women there."

Hearing him admit this made me feel a little better. At least I wasn't the only one who entered this relationship without my virginity.

Then it hit me like a ton of bricks. What if this child wasn't even Jon's? My mind was racing to calculate how long it had been since Garek and I made love. Was it possible?

Meanwhile, Jon started some soup for our supper. This made me feel even more guilty. Here he was being nice to me, but I wasn't sure I deserved it.

***

A couple of weeks later, Jon found a more promising job in another valley. This one was even farther north, but not as high in elevation, so the winters were actually milder. The hardest part for me was having to say good-bye to Calien.

We went into the forest for a picnic on a warm early summer day. I was beginning to lose the morning sickness now, and food was tasting better again.

"I am so glad we could do this," I sighed, lying on the blanket we spread, looking up through the green leaves of the trees overhead. "I'm going to miss you so much, Calien."

"I'm glad you and Jon will have a place to live when you get there." She handed me some soft bread with homemade berry jam on it.

"I just love your berry jam," I said, sitting up and taking a bite, but I found myself sobbing suddenly. "How am I ever going to live without you?"

"Martina, what's wrong?"

"I think I'm pregnant!"

"Isn't that good?"

"Well, I guess."

"You're worried about something, though, aren't you?"

I nodded, but no sound came out of my mouth when I tried to speak.

"Let me guess. You're afraid this child may not be Jon's."

All I could do was nod again.

"How long has it been since you and Garek-"

"Slept together?"

It was her turn to nod.

"About four months. How did you know, anyway?"

"I guess I know you too well, Martina. And I'm thinking you're not sure how far along you are."

"No. We can't afford a doctor right now."

She took my hand.

"The chances are slim, Martina. Odds are in favor of Jon being the father."

"I know. But there's still this little gnawing doubt."

"Just try not to worry about it. What happens will be the Lord's will."

"I sure hope so." Tears came pouring from my eyes again. "So many bad things have happened to my family. My father died—Mother is gone—Stephen was killed."

"But you *have* found Darien again."

"And I have Jael."

"And Jon, who also loves you."

"But I'm afraid of what might happen if it's obvious this baby isn't his."

"Well, there's no way to know that until about five months from now."

I turned to her then, and buried my head on her shoulder.

Gently she stroked my hair. "I'll keep you all in my prayers," she whispered. "You need to try and trust God has a plan here."

"I'll try, Calien."

***

Then we moved north, and I tried to focus on Jon and rebuilding my relationship with him. I told myself I was meant to fit into Jon's world, and tried very hard to settle into life with him again. We still weren't formally married, and I wondered sometimes if he would still want me after all the conflict. I just hoped and prayed that this baby that was coming would somehow heal some of the wounds between us—and not cause another rift.

Sometimes the time seemed to fly by, but other days I found myself on the verge of tears constantly. Once, Calien was able to come up for a visit.

"You look so good," she told me. "I think being a mother is going to suit you."

"I hope so. I've never been one of those people who were drawn to babies. I always wondered if I was ever meant to be a mother."

"Oh, don't worry, Martina. It will all come to you when you need it."

I sincerely hoped she was right. It was hard to tell her good-bye again. In fact, I clung to her, and finally begged, "Please come and help me when the time comes, Calien. I don't have a mother to come."

"Of course, I'll come. Thank you so much for asking me. I'm honored."

***

I went into labor one night in autumn, when the days were getting shorter and winter was touching the mountain peaks. Jon wanted to take me down the road to the hospital, but I refused. Somehow, I couldn't trust doctors very much, after the men in lab coats had taken my mother away.

As first labors go, I'm told I didn't have a very difficult time. But it seemed I was timing contractions forever, until I finally got that uncontrollable urge to push.

My labor lasted for about 12 hours, which gave Calien time to come to my side. By the time I was fully dilated, she was there holding my hand, and encouraging me. It actually felt good to push, after all the grinding pain. Suddenly, everything seemed to move. Then I heard a tiny cry.

"Here she is!" said Calien.

"She's beautiful," Jon's voice came.

I grabbed for his hand.

Calien placed the little girl at my breast, where she nestled gently.

Now all the pain was forgotten. What a miraculous thing to see this new life, right here in my arms! Calien swaddled her in a small blanket, but I pulled the cover off, so I could really see her and hold her against my flesh. She was of my very flesh—and Jon's, I told myself. Looking at her tiny face, I saw her eyes open and look right into mine.

"We should call her Celestia," I said. "Because she has stars in her eyes."

"That's a pretty name," said Calien.

"Yes," said Jon. "Celestia."

***

Now there was no choice but to fall into the life of motherhood. Some days I was totally exhausted, but others were better. One day when Celestia was about three weeks old, there came a chime on the transceiver. Jon was back at his job, so I answered quickly, hoping the sound wouldn't disturb Celestia's nap. I really needed this time to rest, too.

"Martina?" came a strangely familiar voice. "Hi, it's Garek."

"Garek?" I was filled with disbelief. "How did you find me?"

"I have my sources," he laughed. "Congratulations on your new arrival."

"How did you—? *I* know. You have your sources."

"What did you name the baby?" he asked.

"Her name is Celestia. She's really beautiful."

"What does she look like?"

"Well, she has light brown hair, but not very much. Her eyes are very brown. Some babies change eye colors, but I think hers are going to stay brown."

"Jon must have brown eyes," he said.

"Yes, he does." Even as I said this, I remembered Garek's eyes were blue. So now I knew who Celestia's father was, and so did he.

"Martina, I know you're going to be a wonderful mother. Having children is one of the greatest challenges, but also one of the greatest joys in life. Believe me, I know."

"Thanks for calling, Garek. It means a lot to hear from you."

"You're very welcome," he said. Then we signed off, and that was the last I ever heard from him.

Later that day, I took out all his letters and just held them for awhile. I wanted to open them, but my hands seemed to freeze. 'It will be better for everyone if you don't read these again,' I thought. 'And Jon would be hurt, if he ever saw them.' So, I took them to the fireplace and set them on the fire, one by one. 'Good-bye, Garek,' I thought.

I never told Jon that Garek called. I decided it wouldn't make any difference in the long run. But it's always stayed in my heart that he cared enough to call, and ask about Celestia's eyes.

***

Not long after this, it was time for Jael to return to Celeton for the winter. But this time, Jon said we all should go. "I think it will be a better place for the baby through the winter, too."

I was relieved he said this, because I knew our drafty cabin might not be the best place for a baby. I knew Jon and Darien didn't always get along in the same house, but I hoped this time would be different.

Once we got there and settled in, things did seem better than before, and it was also good to be with Jael for the winter.

Jon found work at a warehouse loading crates and boxes. He always seemed to find some way to support us, and I was very proud of him for this. I could tell, too, how much he loved our daughter. She was the light of his world.

One winter day, he and Darien came home at the same time, which was not usual. I was feeding Celestia at the time, so I pulled a blanket over me, since I didn't want to embarrass anyone.

"I think it's time that we started looking for it," Jon was saying. "I know it's been a long time, but still, it *is* the reason we came."

"Yes, I know it'll be good for Martina and Jael," said Darien, as they came into the living room.

"Looking for what?" I asked.

"The Fountain," said Darien, turning to me.

"But how can I go now—with Celestia?"

"Jon and I have been talking, and thinking that maybe he can cross a GAP, to make the trip shorter."

"But do you know where to go?" I was beginning to get excited at the idea. After all, I still had a lot of guilt and dirt in my soul to deal with. Jon had no idea how much.

"Well, it'll depend on what Feier finds," said Jon.

"You sent him out, without Jael knowing?"

"Don't worry, we talked to Jael," Darien smiled. "And Feier is already back."

Just then, Feier and Jael were walking into the room.

"What is this," I asked, "A family council? I guess I'm glad you didn't leave me out."

CHAPTER 17

MANY WATERS

["Ginna," came a familiar voice in her mind.

"Danny, is that really you?"

"Sure is! Jael and Jon just brought me back. It feels good to be 'within' Jael again. How are you doing?"

"Oh, I'm fine," she mentally shrugged. Actually, she was feeling somewhat confused right then, glad Martina had finally decided she belonged with Jon. She liked being with him, too, but that was part of the problem. Sometimes, she knew she was feeling too much for Jon in her own soul.

"So, it looks like we may be setting out on another journey," Danny was saying, in Jael's voice.

"Guess so," she replied with Martina's voice. Then that voice continued:]

We were all gathered around, listening in our minds as Feier shared what he found on his long flight to the city called Tornatoh, three days' journey away by groundcar.

'There are hundreds of tall buildings. One is a tall tower that rises above all else, with a pointed top shining in the sunlight.'

"Sounds like Neptune Spire," said Jael.

'Yes, it looks like it, too.'

"Does this mean Earth is a System planet?" I moaned.

"Oh no," said Darien. "This tower was built very long ago, in ancient times. It's probably where the System got their idea for Neptune Spire, though."

"What else did you see, Feier?" I asked.

'Well, the most magnificent building is one called The Temple of the Way. It shines like gold and sits right beside a huge lake, surrounded by lush green lawns and brightly-colored flower gardens. In the very center of the complex is a fountain that shoots water high into the air. Colors in the fountain change as the waters rise and fall in time to beautiful music. I've never seen anything like it.'

Jael's eyes were wide. "So you found it!"

'It would seem so.'

"This is the largest and most influential city on the planet," Darien added.

"Then it makes sense that the Fountain would be there," nodded Jon.

"Is there any way we can go see it?" I patted Darien on the shoulder, so that he'd think I was asking his permission.

"Let me talk to my Rangers. Perhaps we can find a way. I know how important this is to you, Sis."

"But what about Celestia? I'm not sure it's good for babies to cross the GAP."

"Darien has a plan," said Jon.

I looked from one of them to the other. Apparently, they'd come to some agreement, which was almost a miracle.

"I know a new mother named Atonia, who's willing to be a wet nurse. And if we're fortunate, you won't be gone that long."

The thought of leaving Celestia with someone else made my heart hurt, but I'd waited so long to find this Fountain, the place we'd been told could wash away all our guilt. It was a hard choice.

Jon seemed to understand this, for he came and took my hand. "I'm sure Atonia will take good care of her," he said.

"It's a good thing I've been weaning Celestia to a bottle," I said, "Not just for her sake but mine, too. I'd hate to be all engorged with milk for the whole trip."

Jon gave me a surprised look. I guess he hadn't thought much about what nursing a baby really involved.

The very next day, Darien brought two of his men to meet with us.

"This is Donmal and Soren," he said.

As soon as I looked up, I felt as though I was seeing a

ghost. Donmal looked so much like my brother Stephen, my heart almost stopped beating.

"Is something wrong?" asked Darien.

"Uh, no. Donmal looks so much like Stephen."

Darien smiled, "Oh yeah, I forgot. He's our cousin, you know. His father, Dominic, is Dad's twin brother."

"Really!" I cried. "I had no idea what happened to Dad's brother."

"I met him in the Rebels," said Darien quietly. "Like *our* oldest brother, Donmal was named for his father, too."

I walked over and shook his hand. "I'm really glad to meet you," I said, trying to swallow the lump in my throat. Then I shrugged and threw my arms around him.

"It's good to finally meet you, too." He hugged me back, then turned to Jael when we parted. "And I assume this is Jael." He reached over and patted him on the head.

"Well, now that we're introduced," Darien resumed, "Donmal and Soren have been wanting to see this Temple of the Way, too. I've arranged for all of you to make a pilgrimage there together."

I crossed the room and hugged my brother. "Darien, thanks so much."

Atonia was standing there, too, holding Celestia. Jon and I both shed tears as we kissed her on the forehead and cheeks. "We'll be back soon, baby girl," I whispered.

"I hope all goes well in your search," said Darien. "I looked for the Lord a long time, too."

"But how did you find him?" I asked.

"It's too long a story for right now. You all need to get ready. Be sure to wear your oldest traveling clothes. That will make it look like you've traveled far. And carry only what you need for a day's walk, so you won't look too rich."

"Thank you, Darien," said Jon, stepping up then. They shook hands solemnly.

"Remember, you're pilgrims," Darien stepped toward the door. "And pilgrims aren't permitted any weapons."

After he left, we began to sort our few belongings, trying to decide what was really needed for a day's walk.

"We don't want to take too much and tire ourselves," said Jon.

I decided all I really needed was an extra jacket. Jael did the same, but also insisted on making room in his pack-sack for Feier.

'I could fly,' Feier said. 'There's no need for you to carry my weight.'

"Well, perhaps you can fly part of the time," Jael said.

"Jael is right, Feier," said Jon. "We don't want to look too unusual." There didn't seem to be any feier-cats on Earth.

At last, we were ready. Donmal and Soren rose from their spots near the hearth, and without any more delay Jon drew us into a circle. Closing his eyes, he concentrated on the coordinates and the image in Feier's thoughts of a distant city skyline.

***

As we entered the city proper, there were many groundcars whizzing past on the road. Above our heads, small vehicles buzzed and flew by. Everyone seemed to be in a hurry, but we didn't have any idea where they were going. Fortunately, Soren brought a detailed map of the city. Whenever we reached a junction which we were unsure of, he'd pour over it and tell where he thought we should go next.

When we got into the depths of center-city, however, the signs were harder to find, and the buildings were so tall that it was hard to get our bearings. At last, Jael and Jon agreed to let Feier fly above us, giving the benefit of his 'bird's-eye view,' as he called it. With this help, we finally saw the flashing gold of the Temple of the Way in the distance.

It was situated right on the shore of a bright blue lake whose waters sparkled in the noonday sun. Just as Feier said, we glimpsed waters shooting high into the air, dancing to music that came from hidden speakers somewhere. The only problem we faced now was how to get into the Temple compound.

Donmal took us to what looked like a gated tunnel. Guards at the portcullis challenged us immediately.

"Halt! State your business!"

"We're pilgrims come to experience the cleansing fountains," said Soren.

"At whose invitation have you come?"

'Invitation?' Feier asked.

That was the question in all of our minds.

"Uh—we didn't know we needed invitations—" Jon began.

"Well, you do! Go down High Street, and inquire at the last shop on the right."

With a shrug, we turned and headed in the direction the guards pointed.

"I didn't know about any of this," Soren said.

"Me neither," said Donmal.

"We're not Earth-natives, as you know," said Jon, "So we're clueless."

Jael and I just kept quiet and followed the others.

Soon we were nearing the end of the little side street the guard called High Street. On our right was a tiny shop with dirty windows, not looking very impressive. When we pushed on the grimy door to enter, it made a loud creaking sound.

'They could use some hinge oil,' Feier observed.

"That's the least of what this place needs," said Jon.

The interior of the shop was very dimly lit. We could barely make out a counter in the back of the store, and a man napping in a chair behind it.

"Uh-excuse us!" called Soren.

The figure jerked awake. "Huh?"

"We were told to come here about invitations?" Donmal added.

"Invitations to what?" a scratchy voice asked.

This didn't sound at all promising.

"We're pilgrims come to see the Temple of the Way. The guards said to come see you about invitations," said Soren.

"Ah, so they're trying that ploy again, are they?"

"What do you mean?" asked Jon.

"Oh, different guards have their own scams they run," the shopkeeper replied. "It must be Sircon and Poil on duty this week. They think they can bribe me by sending their business my way."

"What do we have to do then?" Soren was getting impatient.

"So where have you come from?" he asked.

"Does that really matter?" Soren replied gruffly.

"Now listen!" The old cracked voice suddenly became stronger. "You need to do as I ask if you expect me to do anything for you, right?"

"Sorry," said Soren, almost to himself.

"Three of us have come from Terres," Jon put in. "It's a very distant planet beyond the Arcturi system."

The man let out a shrill whistle at this. "So, our fountain is known so far out in the Galaxy?"

"Well, not exactly," Jon continued. "A hermit told us about it. Since then, we've come in many stages. First, we had to find the Centauri Sector, and then the planet Maia—I mean Earth."

"We've been searching a very long time, sir," Jael added, trying to sound respectful.

Soren and Donmal seemed thankful that we took the man's attention, so that they didn't have to reveal anything about themselves.

"And what do you expect to gain from our fountain?"

"We want to be cleansed of all our guilt and mistakes," I spoke up.

The man's eyes turned toward me, and I thought I saw surprise in them. Before I could wonder much about this, he said quickly, "Well, you must try and see."

He reached behind his counter and took out some crumpled currency of different colors, with strange symbols on them.

"These old bills should be enough to satisfy Sircon," he muttered, almost to himself. "Here, give these to the guards you met. Tell them I don't have any more to give."

"Thank you, sir." Soren took the notes and tucked them into a pocket in his tunic.

"Just remember," the man called, as we started for the creaking door. "There are other fountains here on Earth."

As we stepped back into the narrow street, my mind was whirling in confusion. "Other fountains?" Jael was echoing my thoughts. "How can we know which is the right one?"

'I guess we must try and see,' said Feier. 'Like the old man said.'

So, we trudged back up High Street, and turned into the arched entryway. This time the guards just eyed us and nodded in a pleased way when Soren handed them the pile of crumpled notes, giving the old man's message, "He said to tell you that's all he has."

"So he always says," one guard chuckled.

The taller of the two, who seemed to be in charge, turned and opened the portcullis. As we quickly walked through, we heard him say, "Blessings to you, pilgrims."

'Well, I guess we paid enough to get a blessing,' came Feier's thoughts.

"This doesn't seem to me like the way to run a temple for the True King," Jon grumbled.

"Well, maybe we just chose the wrong gate," I said.

No one gave me any reply, so we trudged up the cobblestone walkway in silence. Through a narrow opening, I could hear the splash of water. The fountain was close by.

We all picked up our pace. Soon we turned a corner, and there before us was a glorious sight. Cool waters splashed and played in the sunlight. Colors danced in the drops, some from lights below the water's surface, and some natural rainbows caused by the sunlight and spray.

I set down my pack-sack, and began to take off my shoes. My feet were eager to feel that water. The others were doing the same.

"What do you think you're doing?" a sharp voice called.

A tall man in bright red livery came running up to us. "Who are you?" he demanded.

"We're just humble pilgrims," said Donmal. "We've come to be cleansed by the fountain."

"You can't do that here."

"So where do we need to go?" I tried to ask as respectfully as I could, even though my anger and frustration were getting stronger with every moment.

"You may stand in the mist on that platform." He pointed up some steps that led to a flat area, catching spray from the largest plume of water. It was coming down like a soft rain, in gentle droplets. "Or you can buy your bottle of 'Living Water' at the vendors on Lake Street," he added.

All of us were standing with our mouths open, dumbfounded. We came all this way looking for miraculous waters, and now were told we might have to pay? This was even harder to take than having to bribe the guards at the gate.

Still, we decided to climb the steps and see what was on the platform.

Once we reached it, the platform was revealed to be made of closely-set gray bricks, each with a name engraved on it. The man in red came up close behind us, evidently to supervise our visit to the mist.

"What are the names for, sir?" Jael asked.

"They're people who've given of their treasures," he smiled, "Those grateful for our fountain, who gave to build this platform so all can see the dancing waters."

"But how do we get cleansed of our guilt?" I couldn't help asking. Nothing else really mattered to me.

"Oh, dear! But forgiveness is a process, you see." The man began to gesture in an almost frantic way. "You must perform many rituals, and then you'll be ready to truly receive."

'But Johan said the *waters* would cleanse us,' Feier reminded me.

By this time, we were all standing near the front of the platform where the mist was thickest, getting drenched, clothing and all.

"Do you feel any different, Sis?" I heard Jael ask me.

"Just wet and cold," I said. "What about you, Jon?"

"I'm the skeptic here, Martina. All I feel is damp."

Soren and Donmal were shaking their heads by this time, too. "I guess we could see what this Lake Street looks like," Donmal shrugged.

We picked our way down the steep stairs on the other side of the platform, each with another engraved name on it. "Guess we know how this was paid for," muttered Jon. "Gifts from the faithful."

At the bottom of these stairs, another wider avenue led between two more brightly-colored plumes of water. The one on our right was full of dancing green and gold lights, while the one on the left was in shades of red and blue.

"They *are* beautiful, aren't they?" Jael was trying hard to see the good in everything.

"But I don't feel any different," I said to him in a loud whisper.

Finally, we could see the shore of the lake right in front of us. A row of little shops and kiosks stretched out along the entire walkway that skirted the lake. Between the shops and the water was a wide band of pure white sand. It actually shone in the sun and made my eyes hurt. I noticed Jon trying to shield his eyes with a hand and remembered how he was more sensitive to bright light because of his early childhood on Rubicon, a planet dimly lit by a distant red sun.

"I guess this is Lake Street," Donmal was saying.

"What else?" Soren's voice was beginning to sound as discouraged as I felt.

As we walked along, various shopkeepers were hawking their wares, everything from little bottles of 'Holy Fountain Water' to strings of crystal, rainbow-colored beads. "Infused with the true colors of the Fountain!" sellers called. "Take the power of the waters home to your families!"

'This isn't at all what I expected.' Feier sounded apologetic.

"Or what any of us expected," Jon replied. "Don't feel so bad. It's not your fault."

By now, we were walking into the ornamental gardens Feier mentioned before. They were full of so many kinds of plants and flowers that it was hard to identify even half of them. Fortunately for the curious, there were small signs at the base of the plants, identifying them and their origin. Most were from Earth, the signs told us, but some were brought by pilgrims from distant planets. We didn't find anything from Terres or any of the other planets we'd visited in our journeys, though.

"I guess no one from our end of the Galaxy has been here," Jon shrugged.

"Or they're like us, and didn't bring any plants," said Jael.

"Yeah. We had no idea," I said.

'I wonder if these are true samples from other planets or if someone just make these names up to be impressive?' Feier, as usual, was questioning what he saw.

"Feier has a point," Jon said. "Who would ever know?"

"We're really getting cynical now, aren't we?" Jael nodded at me.

"I think it's time to go," Soren said just then.

"I guess so. There's nothing for us here," I sighed.

Once we were through the thick walls surrounding the Temple area, we all sighed again with disappointment. "I thought we were so close," said Jael.

"This place is just a money-making enterprise," Jon added.

"I wonder what the old man meant about there being other fountains," said Donmal.

"I think we should go back and ask him. How about the rest of you?"

"I agree with Martina," he said, nodding my way.

So, we worked our way back around the perimeter of the Temple walls, finally getting back to High Street. The shop at the end of the row looked just like before. I realized the owner kept the creaky door so he could hear if anyone came in.

Sure enough, when we reached the counter in the back of the tiny, crowded shop, he was sitting up waiting for us this time.

"So, my pilgrims, what did you think?"

"It was a big fake!" said Jael.

"It wasn't what we expected," Jon agreed.

"Then I can see you *are* true seekers," he smiled. "Most don't come back. They buy their beads and vials and go home feeling better about themselves."

"What we're seeking is the fountain that truly can cleanse us," I added. Every time I said this, I could feel the need growing within me. Would I ever find any release from this weight of guilt I carried?

"Yes, I see that's true," he nodded.

"Are you going to send us to another place that needs bribes and donations?" said Soren.

"Oh, no." The old man's eyes were dancing now. "I'm

going to tell you to leave this corrupted city. And don't go to any of the other so-called great cities of Earth. Each one claims to have the True Fountain, but none of them do. Go into the desert that's far to the east. This is where the True Fountain is, and you'll know it by its thick red water. It won't look like a fountain that can cleanse, but it does. The world is full of paradoxes, and this is the greatest one of all. Have you not read in The Book? 'The stone the builders rejected has become the capstone.' And 'He had no beauty that we should desire him.' You may not understand now, but you will then."

We were shaking our heads at his words. Jael, however, was paging through his Book again, trying to find the passages the old man quoted. I realized he must have stuffed it in his pack-sack when none of us were looking.

"Look in the book called *Isaiah*, young one," the old man said. "That prophet has many words of wisdom, even in our time. I see you'll be a great help to all you meet in life. The Book is meant to be read. The rest of you can learn from this young lad's example." His eyes seemed to bore into each of us, as he spoke.

Jael looked up into the man's eyes for an instant, and a flash of light seemed to pass between them. I blinked and looked again, but then it was gone.

"So, how do we find this desert?" Jon asked.

"You must take the east road out of the city, my son, past the second large lake you see. Then you'll cross a range of mountains, and on their eastern side, you'll find a desert. There you must travel by night, for the days will scorch you to dust. Also, by night you'll be able to follow the star. It will be the brightest light in the east, and it won't move across the sky, as the other stars do with the passage of the night. Keep it in your sight, and after several days, you'll find the True Fountain."

"Thank you, sir," Donmal said quickly. Then he turned to the rest of us. "We must report to Darien first, though."

We were all anxious to set out on that eastern road, but knew he was right. We needed to let Darien know what we'd found. And so, Jon took us back to the Safe House.

***

Darien could see the disappointment in our eyes, even before we began telling him our story. His eyes grew even sadder as we continued. At last, when all of us had put in our own observations, he sighed, "So even the people of Earth have strayed from the truth. It's so sad to think they had the King in their very midst many times through history, and yet they still go after false gods."

"It seems like everywhere we go, the false gods are in control," said Jael.

"Or the evil spirits." I added.

"Darien, perhaps you should tell us how *you* found the True King—before we go stumbling off on another futile journey." Jon was looking Darien in the eye.

"All right. I was in the Inland Raiders, as you know. I felt sure the Rebels were the problem, and once we'd defeated them, the System would sort things out. I knew from Father there was a True King, and he came to a place called Earth, long ago in history, but I wasn't sure what it had to do with me. One day, a fellow soldier in my company quietly and secretly gave me a small digital player called a 'corder. All I needed to do was put an earbud in, and I could hear the words of The Book being read to me.

"It was so much easier than trying to read during that time in my life. I had a small portion of The Book in my pack, but it seemed when there was time, there wasn't enough light, or I was just too tired. But with this 'corder, I could listen while I was resting, even waiting to fall asleep.

"The stories in The Book began to make more sense to me. I understood that it truly was the Lord God who made the Universe. No one who was not all-powerful could have designed such an intricate system."

"Just like we learned when we talked with Johan," Jael said.

"Then I heard how God sent his son to Earth, to pay the price for all of humankind's evils. It seemed unbelievable anyone could care enough to do such a thing for wandering human beings. But the words were right there,

'For God so loved the world that he gave his one and only Son, that whoever believes in him should not perish, but have everlasting life'."

"The Book says that?" Jael pulled his copy out.

"Look in the book called *John*—I think it's chapter three," Darien smiled. "That's how I learned this God cared about me and sent his Spirit to help me believe all these things. So, I just prayed to him, asking him to forgive me for my unbelief. I know he changed me, because since I prayed that prayer, things have been different. Oh, I still make mistakes, but I ask the Lord to guide me and help me do what pleases him."

"You didn't ever really find the Fountain?" Jon asked.

"Not physically. But I think I did spiritually, when I prayed and asked God to forgive me for the sake of what his Son had done."

"I've read that story about the Son's death and resurrection," Jael said. "But I didn't realize it had a meaning for me personally."

"The whole point of the crucifixion is that Kristos, God's son, died in my place," said Darien. "He had no guilt of his own, so he took mine—and yours, and everyone's—on himself. That's why The Book says, 'By his wounds, we are healed'."

"Boy, that's sure a lot to take in," Jon muttered.

"This is why some people go to find the Fountain," said Darien. "It gives a physical reality to everything."

"Well, I guess I'm one of those people," said Jon.

"Me too," I said. "You know, Darien," I stepped up and laid my hand on his shoulder, "When we were growing up, you seemed like the one who always had to have proof, always asking questions. But now here you are living by faith—and *I* have all the questions."

"It's all right, Sis," he smiled. "But I hope now you see that even someone like me can believe."

"So, do we have your permission to search for this Fountain in the Desert?" Soren asked.

"You do, Soren, but I need Donmal here in the city."

Donmal looked disappointed, but gave a quick salute to his commander.

"I have word of your father," Darien added.

Donmal stopped short and looked very surprised. "I thought he was still on Terres."

"He was the last I knew, but my sources tell me he was wounded in the Battle of Alpha Centauri."

"How is he?" Donmal seemed afraid to ask the obvious question.

"He's recovering well, I'm told. But I think it would be good for you to be here in the city when he arrives."

"Yes, sir," he said quickly. Now he knew his commander was doing *him* a favor, instead of the reverse.

"Darien, will you come with us to the Fountain—to see it for yourself?" Jael asked.

"No, I can't. I'm needed here, too. But I'll take your word for it," he smiled.

CHAPTER 18

CRYING IN THE WILDERNESS

Jon didn't have the coordinates for the desert the old man told us about. Our only bearings were the city of Tornatoh, so we had to go back there when we crossed the GAP. I cried for hours at the thought of leaving Celestia again, but if I really wanted to find the Fountain, we could see no other choice.

As we walked, the skyline of the city gradually sank below the horizon. The farther we headed into the east, the drier the terrain became. At first, we skirted the shore of a large blue lake. Soren thought the name of it was Huo. After the first day's travel, we crossed a low ridge, and from the top, we could see the next lake the old man mentioned. It was full of whitecaps, for the winds were high.

"What is this lake called, do you know?" I asked Soren.

"My map says it's Omato Lake."

Between these two lakes flowed a river. We could see it dashing itself over rocks, and occasionally it went over a drop large enough to make a waterfall.

"That river is beautiful." Jael was looking through a pair of spyglasses Darien gave him.

"I'm glad we don't have to cross it or try to take a boat down it," said Jon.

Soren nodded. Then he pointed to the eastern horizon that loomed out of the haze beyond Omato Lake. "There are the Cruax Mountains."

"That's a strange name," said Jael.

"All the names are strange here," I sighed.

Jael focused his spyglasses on the distant mountains. "They look a lot like the Peaks on Terres. I can even see snow on the highest ridges."

"Let me see, please." I stepped close enough to grab the spyglasses, but then stopped my hand. Jael looked over at me and smiled.

"Here." He handed the glasses to me. "Thanks for not grabbing."

I felt sort of sheepish, though, because I *had* almost grabbed them. What was I anyway, some little child? My younger brother seemed more mature than I was.

Then my breath stopped in my throat as I focused the glasses on those distant peaks. They were amazing, seeming to tower straight up in the sky, with few foothills before them. At their base was a wide, green valley, and I could make out at least two small turquoise lakes sitting at the foot of the steep rocky slopes.

"Do we have to cross those?" Jon was looking over

Soren's shoulder at the map.

"No, we can skirt around to the south. There's a pass there."

"That's good. So where is this desert?"

"It appears to be east of the pass." Soren was pointing to a spot colored orange on the map.

I handed the glasses back to Jael and joined them. "What does that symbol mean?" I pointed to a black plus sign in the center of that orange area. "I saw it on some Rebel uniforms."

"Oh, that's the cross," Soren smiled. "It is the sign of the True King, and yes, we Rebels wear it proudly. It symbolizes all the King has done for us. You see, he died on a rough wooden cross, set up in the ground, when he took our guilt away."

"He what?" This still seemed beyond my understanding.

"The people of the great city of that time—it was called Jerusalem—nailed him to a large timber cross. It was the most terrible form of execution ever devised by humans, they say." Soren's voice was full of reverence, so I could tell this was a serious subject to him.

Jael joined us. "But wasn't he God's son? Couldn't he have stopped them?"

"Of course, he could have," Soren said. "But he chose not to. He chose to die for me—you, all of us."

"But why?" I was still feeling confused.

'Remember what Darien said?' came Feier's thought then. 'It was the only way to pay the price for all the guilt of humans.'

"He's right, you know." Soren turned toward Feier, as he spoke. So he could hear Feier, too. "He could have called down an army of angels, but instead he died alone."

"That's awful." I felt my throat tightening. "Why would he do that? I feel overwhelmed sometimes about just my own mistakes. How must the guilt of the whole world have felt to him?"

"He did it for love." Soren folded his hands and bowed his head. "The Book says, 'For God so loved the world'…"

"Darien told us that, too," I said. "And so did Johan. Remember? He called it the Mystery of Love."

"Yes," Jael said. "And look at this verse I just found, 'Greater love has no one than this—that he lay down his life for his friends'."

"And then three days later," Soren went on, "He proved he was God by rising from the dead."

"Wow—the resurrection!" mouthed Jael. "Now I see why it's so important."

"Well, I'm still confused. I *really* need to see this Fountain," I said. "Let's get going."

***

The valley below the Cruax Mountains looked fairly flat, but as we left the last of the lakeshore and began to cross it, we found it rose and fell in many gentle swales. It only looked flat in comparison to those towering peaks.

As we moved past the fringes of the valley, we encountered thickets of low-growing shrubs. Soren said he thought they were a kind of willow. In some places, they hid wet places we found only after we stepped in them. Our boots and leggings were soon soaking wet.

"Ugh! My feet are soaked, and now my toes feel frozen." I hated to be the first to complain, but I couldn't force myself to suffer in silence any longer.

"The water in this valley comes right off the snow and glaciers up there." Soren pointed to the white areas on the mountainsides. "So it's pretty icy."

"Well, my feet are ice now." I moaned.

Jon stopped for a moment and shaded his eyes, looking toward a low rise to our left. "Perhaps that will be a dry spot." He pointed, as he turned to Soren. "Maybe we should take a short break."

"Sounds good to me." Both Soren and I spoke in unison, and then began to laugh.

When we reached the rise, it proved to be very rocky but dry. We dropped our pack-sacks beside the rocks, and stretched ourselves out to gather in as much warm sun as we could. There was a fresh wind still blowing, but I found if I laid myself out close to the ground, I felt warmer. From this vantage point, I discovered there were dozens of tiny colored flowers poking up between the rocks.

"Look at all these flowers." I pointed to some little blue ones beside me. "They have a tough place to call home. But they're smart. They grow low to the ground where it's warmer and not so windy."

'That's where I have an advantage,' came Feier's voice in our minds. 'I'm lower to the ground than any of you.'

"I swear that if that feier-cat could laugh, he would be," said Jon, chuckling a little himself.

"Well, he *is* always smiling." I pointed to the creature's upturned mouth.

"So that's why you keep him around?" asked Soren.

Jon laughed out loud at this. "Yeah, he's good for a laugh."

"Hey! Don't make fun of Feier—he's really smart." Jael sounded offended.

"Sorry, Jael." I patted him on the arm, and then rubbed Feier's head. "We're just trying to make ourselves feel better. Laughing does warm you up!"

Just then, I looked toward the west and realized the sun was low on the horizon. "What are we going to do for the night?" I turned to Soren.

"I have two tents in my gear," he replied. "I think we can find a spot for them sheltered from the wind, just past those rocks up there." He pointed toward another rise not far above us.

"How should we split up for sleeping?" I saw Jon glance at me when he said this, and knew exactly what he was thinking.

"I'll go with Jael," I said quickly, before anyone could suggest anything else. "We'll have Feier with us for protection."

"Sounds reasonable," said Soren. "Jon can bunk with me."

Even though Jon and I would have liked to be together, it seemed better for Jael to be with me, than with a comparative stranger. It wasn't that I didn't trust Soren—I just felt my little brother was still my responsibility.

"Can we eat something before we set up tents?" I asked. "I'm famished."

"I think we should get the tents up while we still have light," Jon said. "Then we can eat."

Soren nodded. 'Well, the men have decided—this time,' I thought to myself.

Once we got ourselves over the next rise, we found an almost level spot in the shelter of some large boulders. The small, nylon tents billowed in the wind at first, but once they were properly staked, they held steady. When I crawled inside one to spread out sleeping mats, I could hear the steady, whipping sound the wind made with the ropes and tent fabric. I hoped the noise wouldn't keep me awake all night.

After we finished with this set-up, Jael and I settled our gear in our tent. Then I pulled the small gas stove out of my pack. There were four tins of soup, but after weighing them in my hands, I decided I'd warm only two, with no idea how many more meals we'd need before we found another food source. By the time Jon and Soren had the other tent up, there were four small cups of warm soup ready.

"This really hits the spot," Soren smiled at me across the top of his cup.

I suddenly realized that I seldom saw him smile. Now I could see dark curls peeking out the edges of the hat he always wore. It was a grayish-green that made him harder to see in the distance, a good color for a Rebel to wear, I thought. Then I noticed his clothing was the same drab color.

Jon, Jael, and I were wearing what I salvaged of our Redlark bark-clothes. Most of the fabric was patched in several places, so our camouflage wasn't as good as before. Besides, we weren't in the Wilds of Terres anymore, so the vegetation colors were slightly different.

Once the soup was gone, I rinsed out the cups with a little water. Instead of draining out the water, though, each of us drank it from our own cup. We didn't want to waste anything.

As the sky darkened, a few stars began to appear. After putting the cooking gear away, I sat outside the door of my tent, watching as more stars came out, with Jael cuddled up beside me.

"Remember how Jon told us the stars are always out there shining, Sis?"

"Sure do." For a brief instant, I could sense he was

also Danny, and I was Ginna, his older sister. In a sense we were, because they were experiencing this with us, as part of us.

"During the day, the light of the sun drowns them out. But once it sets, we can see them reappearing," he continued.

"Do you recognize any patterns in the stars?" I wasn't sure why I asked this, but somewhere deep inside I thought Danny and Ginna would recognize Earth constellations unfamiliar to me.

There was silence for a long time, and then a small voice spoke. "Look toward the north. See that square (actually more of a trapezoid) of stars? It's sort of like a cup or a pan. If you look closely, you can see three stars that come off it to make a handle. Do you see it?"

"Yes," I whispered.

"Now at the top end of the pan, away from the handle, trace an imaginary line off to the right. Do you come to a star right in line with the pan's edge?"

"I think I see one. It's sort of dim."

"That's Polaris, the North Star. It always shows where north is. If you follow down from it, you'll see it's on the end of the handle of another smaller pan."

"Yes!" My voice became more excited. "It's like the two pans are pouring toward each other."

"That's the Big Dipper and the Little Dipper," the small voice said.

I found my voice had nearly left me. I slipped my arm around Jael's shoulder. "Thanks, Danny," I whispered.

"No problem, Sis."

***

A loud crashing sound woke me in the early dawn. I sat bolt upright and cried, "What's that?" before I was even aware of what I was doing.

"It's got to be a big animal of some kind," came Jael's excited voice.

I could hear the men in the other tent clambering out of their sleeping mats.

"Whoa!" came Soren's voice.

"Yeah, what sort of animal is that?" added Jon.

Jael and I peeked out our tent door carefully. Across the ravine we crossed yesterday, we saw a large black-brown animal. It seemed the size of a pack animal, like ones we'd seen on Pyrrhia. But this one had some kind of growths coming from its forehead. When it shook its head, they looked like large menacing branches.

"It's a moose!" came a cry from Jael. I could tell he was still drawing on Danny's memories.

"What's that?" I asked.

"A moose is in the deer family, but it's much larger and more dangerous."

"Should we try to kill it for meat?" I heard Jon's voice ask.

"It would be too much weight to carry," Soren's voice

replied. "I'd hate to waste so much. Still, we do need food. We have several days' trek ahead, from what I can see."

As he was talking to Jon, Soren pulled a short spear from beside his sleeping-mat. Where had he kept that hidden? He motioned for us to keep quiet, and then he crept behind a series of boulders, working his way closer to the huge animal.

Strangely, the moose turned away from us now and appeared to be grazing in some of the willows we trekked through yesterday. Soren was able to get within throwing distance without much trouble. I began to wonder if he could throw the spear hard enough to kill such a large animal. Then I saw him draw even closer, to where he could use his body weight to his best advantage. Rather than throwing the spear, he pushed downward with all his strength while standing on a boulder just above the moose.

The animal gave out a loud bellow and tossed those menacing horns. Soren ducked out of the way just in time. Picking up a fist-sized rock, he brought it down on the beast's head with as much force as he could muster. He repeated this several times, until at last the animal fell and didn't get up again.

We crept cautiously over to see his kill.

"He was so beautiful," murmured Jael.

"But scary, too," I said.

"There's lots of good meat here, but we need to get with it," Soren said.

"Here's a knife. I'll get more out of the cooking gear." I handed my pocket knife to Jon.

He looked surprised I had a knife in my pocket, but I just smiled, "Hey, a girl has to defend herself sometimes."

We spent almost the whole day on the moose. Soren and Jon cut off the best portions of meat, while Jael, Feier, and I kept a smoky fire going. Strips of meat were hung on a rack to dry in the smoke. Feier was the one who came up with the idea for the tripod base that kept the rack from falling over.

As evening fell again, we could hear low moaning sounds in the distance.

"I think the wolves have scented our moose," Soren said. "We need to get our smoked food up where they can't reach it."

There were a few scraggly trees not far from our camp, where Soren and Jon managed to get the meat into their branches. Then they dragged what was left of the moose as far from our camp as they could.

"There, hope that will keep them busy, and they won't think we look like dinner, too," said Jon.

I was surprised at how much Jon seemed to know about life in the wild, but then I realized he'd been with the Redlarks much longer than I had.

It was a long night, though—no matter what precautions we took. We lay as still as we could in our tiny tents, listening to the howls and growls of the wolves, as they fought over and feasted on the remainder of our kill. There was nothing else we could do, except wait for morning—to see if they had left anything of our smoked meat for us.

When dawn finally came, the light seemed grayer than the days before. Sure enough, when I cautiously peeked out our door, I saw nothing but low fog all around us. There were no sounds from where the carcass had lain.

"Jon!" I hissed toward the other tent.

"What?" came his muffled reply.

"Did they leave us any?"

"Don't know yet. Want to come look with me?"

The last thing I felt like doing was crawling out of my warm bed into that cold mist, sneaking over to see if a pack of wolves was feasting on our meat. But I'd asked.

"Okay. I'm coming."

I pulled on every article of clothing I had with me and crept to the door of their tent. Jon seemed surprised I came so quickly, and was still pulling on a tunic and sweater, as he crawled out the door.

"Good morning, sunshine," he grinned at me.

"No sunshine here."

"Well, I always see sunshine in your eyes," he said.

I couldn't think of a quick reply, so I just smiled at him.

We moved slowly, partly due to the fog, and partly so we wouldn't disturb any creatures who might still be about. I was getting disoriented in the mist, but then suddenly I could see the trees. Our carefully wrapped bundles were still hanging where we put them.

Just then, though, I heard a gruff grunting sound off to my right.

"What was that?" I grabbed Jon's arm.

He turned with me, and through the mist there seemed to come a black mountain.

"It's a bear!" His shout must have frightened it, because it turned away from us and seemed to want to climb one of our trees.

"No!" I shouted. Waving my arms, I dashed toward the bear. "Get out of here. Shoo!"

Once again, the bear let out a groaning grunt. Then it turned and ran off into the fog.

"Martina, you're crazy!" Jon grabbed me then.

"Well, he left, didn't he?"

Jon pulled me into his own version of a bear-hug. "You didn't need to risk yourself like that for a bunch of moose meat."

I was surprised to hear what sounded like fear in his voice.

"I'm all right," I whispered into his ear. "Everything is all right."

He pulled me even closer then and began to kiss me gently. I guess it was the eeriness of the fog, and the adrenaline still flowing from the encounter with the bear, but I felt like I just melted. I was totally helpless there in his arms. No words came, but we just went on from the kisses that worked down my neck. I was glad we were concealed from other eyes by the dense fog.

"Please just hold me," I whispered.

Then we were on the ground.

The next thing I knew, we were lying side by side, just trying to catch our breath.

He gently rubbed my back. Then his words came with a sigh, "I love you so much, Martina. I want to be your one and only."

"You mean like The Book talks about, 'One flesh'?"

"Yes."

"I finally understand that now, Jon." I pulled him closer.

"So, you're willing to get married?"

"I think so."

"Why did you keep saying you were unworthy of me?"

"Because you're a good man, and I've just let myself be used by too many others."

"That's all past now. And who says I'm worthy of *you*, either?"

"If we can truly be cleansed by this Fountain, then the past really *will* be over," I sighed. "We can begin again, and nothing else will matter."

"Whatever happens, from now on I'll always be yours," he whispered into my hair.

"I promise to be yours, too, Jon."

***

We shared the extra weight of the smoked meat when we packed up that morning. It was heavy, but the thought of having the extra food made it worth the effort. Feier insisted Jael didn't have to carry him anymore. In fact, he told us how to strap one of the packets of meat onto his back, so it rested securely beneath his wings.

'This way, I can still take off, if I need to.'

Soren made sure of our heading, and then we set out again.

The meat we were able to carry lasted about five days. We tried to eat sparingly, but the hike over the pass was strenuous, even though it was much lower than the rest of the terrain in the Cruax Mountains. It's doubtful we could have made the trip without that moose meat to sustain us.

Despite our encounter in the mist, neither Jon nor I suggested changing the sleeping arrangements. I kept thinking he'd bring it up, and when he didn't, I began to wonder if he was expecting me to. I liked being with Jael, though. There were other moments, like that first night under the stars, when we could feel the presence of Ginna and Danny with us. It still seemed right for us to be together.

The day we ate the last of the moose was the day we left the green lands and entered the bare oranges and browns of the desert. The sun beat down in scorching heat, just like the old man on High Street said.

So, we began to travel by night and tried to rest in the heat of the day, which was very difficult. Most of the time, I lay in the tent with as few clothes on as possible, just resting. Sleep rarely came, except when I was totally exhausted. Again, Jon didn't say a word about changing the sleeping arrangements.

One good thing about traveling by night was we could see the star in the east the old man told us about. It was always low on the horizon just after the sun set in the west. Like the North Star Danny pointed out to Jael and me, it didn't roam across the sky, but seemed to hold itself steady there in the east, sort of like a beacon lamp showing us the way to go.

CHAPTER 19

THE FOUNTAIN IN THE DESERT

I lost track of how many nights we were trekking when we came upon another old man. He was moving in our direction, but slowly, leaning heavily on a gnarled walking stick.

"Hallooo!" he said, as we drew close to him. "Where are you pilgrims bound?"

"We're going to the Fountain in the Desert," said Soren, when we came up to him. "Where else would anyone be going in this wasteland?"

The old man's eyes flashed at this, and he just grinned.

"We are pilgrims, as you've said, he continued. "My name is Soren. This is Jon, Martina, Jael, and Feier." He pointed to each of us in turn.

"Eli is my name," he said. His breath seemed to come in wheezes. "I can see Feier is an animal familiar. Does he speak to any of you?"

"All of us," I said quickly.

"Most interesting," he grinned. "Jael and Martina are siblings, I can see."

"How do you know that, sir?" I asked.

"I can see your family resemblance."

"Jon here—hmm—he has strong feelings for both of you, but especially Martina."

Jon's cheeks began to blush.

"And I believe Soren is your guide."

"How can you tell all that?" Jael asked.

"I've been long years on this Earth," he said, "And learned to read many signs."

"Do you know how far it is to the Fountain, sir?" I could tell Soren was trying to sound as respectful as possible.

"Ah—yes, the Fountain." Then suddenly he began to sing, his old voice wavering and cracking, but still the words came through:

"There is a fountain filled with blood, drawn from the Savior's veins.

And sinners plunged beneath that flood, lose all their guilty stains."

"A fountain filled with blood—that sounds disgusting!" I said, thinking out loud.

"Yes, I suppose it does," Eli nodded. "The water is really just water, but it looks blood-red. It is what it *means* that really matters, though."

"So what *does* it mean?" Soren seemed to be the one who felt the most urgency now. I wondered if this was so he could be finished with us, or if he really wanted to find the Fountain, too.

"Let's continue our journey while I tell," said Eli. "We must keep following the star in the east."

He began to walk again, leaning heavily on his staff. All of us slowed our pace so we could hear what he was saying.

"As you know, the Lord of the Universe sent his Son, who some call Kristos, to this planet Earth. Back then it was the only home of humans. And these humans made a mess of everything because of their pride and willful ways. The only way to set things right was for a sacrifice to be made by someone who was totally pure. There was no human who could do that, and so the Son of God became a true human, and made the sacrifice of himself."

"On the cross," said Soren, reverently.

"Yes. And for the long ages since, some have believed in this sacrifice, but many haven't. To some, it seems too simple to accept what someone else has done for them. They dream up other things they must do to be worthy."

"Like buying bricks for the Temple of the Way?" I asked.

"That and many other things humans do to make themselves feel holy."

"Doesn't The Book say someday Kristos will return to Earth in all his glory?" Jael said.

"Indeed," Eli smiled then. "You've read even to the back of The Book."

Jael nodded, smiling a little.

"That's very good," Eli continued. "All of you should read this Book more, like our young friend does. Yes, Kristos will return and bring a new Earth into being when the time comes. But it's not yet. The Book tells us 'No one knows the day or the hour—only the Father in Heaven.' Through the years, many have tried to guess this time and failed. Great disappointments have been the result of such speculations.

"The only thing I know for sure is the Lord has caused this Fountain in the Desert to appear in my time. Some pilgrims—like you—find in it what they're seeking. Others have no need to come all this way, but accept on faith what The Book and Kristos have revealed to them."

"Like our brother, Darien," I said.

Jon was silent all this time, listening carefully. I could see there was confusion in his mind. Finally, he stepped closer to Eli, and put his hand on the old man's, where it rested on the walking staff.

"Sir?" he began. "I seem to always be the doubter. How can I know any of this is true and not just myths someone invented long ago?"

Eli smiled at him. "I believe this Fountain is here for people such as you, my son."

"How much further is it?" Jael asked.

Eli hadn't answered this question when Soren asked it earlier, so I wondered if he would this time. He stepped around Jon very slowly, raised his staff, and pointed it toward the distant eastern horizon, as the stars were beginning to dim with the sunrise.

"See that tall red rock there?"

We all looked at the cliffs, now beginning to be lit by the rising sun.

"Yes," said Jon.

"That's the Lone Rock. The Fountain is there." Suddenly his eyes closed and he began to chant in a low voice:

"See I am doing a new thing! Now it springs up; do you not perceive it? I am making a way in the desert and streams in the wasteland. . . to give drink to my people, my chosen, the people I formed for myself that they may proclaim my praise."

"What song is that, sir?" asked Jael.

"You'll find it in The Book, in *Isaiah,* my child."

"Do you think we can make it to the rock, if we continue walking into the day?" Soren asked.

"I wouldn't advise it. The days here are scorching. Rest this day, and we'll resume at sunset."

With this, he sat down and began to arrange the folds of his robe into a tent which he used to cover himself. Before long, his breathing came in the steadiness of one asleep.

"How did he do that?" Jon said.

"Beats me," said Soren. "Let's get the tents up."

Soon, all of us were lying in our tents, waiting to see if any sleep would visit *us* this day.

***

I was dreaming of clear sparkling water. I could still hear the sound as I gradually moved from sleep to waking. Then the sounds changed to words. An old man's voice was singing words I'd heard my father sing long ago when I was small:

"Beneath the Cross of Kristos, I long to take my stand—
The shadow of a mighty rock within a weary land;
A home within the wilderness, a rest along the way,
From the burning of the noontime heat, and the burden of the day."

"Martina," came Jael's voice. "Do you remember this song?"

I nodded. "Father sang it a lot."

"It's strange, I can hardly remember Father," he said. "But I do remember the songs."

"It sure fits where we are right now, doesn't it?"

"Yeah. Especially 'the burning of the noontime heat'."

I crept toward the tent door, and pushed it gently open. "The sun is setting now. Let's start packing up."

As we crawled out of our tent, we saw the others were doing the same. Eli, who was still singing softly, was sitting on a flat rock just above our campsite. He appeared to be meditating, with his hands folded across his knees.

I desperately wanted to ask him about the song, but didn't feel it would be right to interrupt him. Still, I found myself walking slowly in his direction. He must have heard my footfalls, for he looked up as soon as I came near.

"Please forgive me, sir." I said. "I heard your song. Where did it come from? My father used to sing it to me."

"Beneath the Cross?"

"Yes, that one. The part about the shadow of a mighty rock really seems to be about the place we're going."

"It does, yes. These words were written eons ago, long before the Fountain was discovered, though."

"How strange. I wonder if the writer ever knew." I sat down beside him. The rock was still very warm from the sun's heat, although the air around us was cooling rapidly, with the sun setting.

"No. I'm sure the song writer was thinking of how he felt in his own life."

"Sir, are you a prophet, like the men Jael reads about in The Book?"

He chuckled for a moment. "No, my child. I'm just a voice."

"A voice?"

"Yes, 'The voice of one crying in the wilderness, make straight the way of the Lord.' Jael can find it for you in The Book. It's the mission the Lord has given me—to help those like you."

"I keep hoping I'll find out what I'm supposed to do

in my life," I sighed. "I keep seeking but never seem to find."

"You're young," he smiled. "You'll find out as you go along. Sometimes, it's only afterwards, as we look back, that we can see we've been on the path the Lord had for us."

"But I wish I could know now. Then I wouldn't make so many mistakes or wrong turns along the way."

"Ah, but the mistakes are ways we learn—often things we can learn no other way."

Jon was walking toward us then. I could see all the gear was packed and ready, so I helped Eli to his feet.

"I'm sorry I interrupted your meditation," I said.

"Oh no, you didn't," he smiled. "I was praying the Lord would give me words to say that might help you."

"Then, perhaps your prayers were answered," I smiled.

***

It actually took us two more nights' walking to reach the Lone Rock. As we drew near, late in the second night, the eastern sky was beginning to brighten. Some days there was very little color in the sky, and the burning yellow sun seemed to just leap into the air. But today, with the rock providing more foreground, the lights of sunrise seemed ready to put on a show for our eyes.

First came hints of red tinging the undersides of low clouds on the horizon. Then these brightened to gold.

Soon streaks and beams of light shot up from the horizon, and finally the edge of the sun's disc began to appear.

"Martina!" Jael cried suddenly. "There's a golden cross in the sky!"

We looked where he pointed, and were all speechless in wonder. It seemed like a miracle. One of the vertical rays intersected a horizontal cloud, whose underside was glowing with golden sunlight. It formed a large and perfect cross.

"Wow," whispered Soren. "So that's why the cross is on my map."

All of us stopped walking, wanting to watch the sunrise without any other distractions. None of us moved until the bright disc of the sun emerged fully above the horizon.

"The Lord is inviting us to the Rock today," Eli said softly. "Not everyone sees it quite this way. 'The Spirit and the Bride say come'."

"Is that in The Book?" Jael asked.

"Absolutely. Look at the very end of The Book. Come, I'll take you to the water that comes from the spiritual Rock, which is Kristos."

Silently, we followed him toward that tall spire standing lonely sentinel in the desert. Though we'd seen it on the horizon for over two days and nights, it seemed to loom higher and higher above us, growing ever redder in the light of the sun.

When we reached the base, Eli tapped with his staff, until a rock dropped off the face in front of him. Suddenly a narrow set of steps was revealed. As he started up these, we followed close behind him. Right in front of me, I could see Feier riding in his favorite spot on Jael's shoulder. This reminded me he'd been very quiet these past couple of nights, but we all were, actually. Something about Eli's presence seemed to make us more introspective.

We soon reached the top of the steps, and a path spread out in both directions. Eli turned to the right without hesitation, and we again followed. The rock above rose steeply now, and long parallel cracks ran up into the dawn sky above us. There was no vegetation along this part of the path.

Then the path took a sharp turn to the left, and I could see sprays of greenery peeking out of a cleft in the rock. A whiff of cool moisture touched my cheek. Eli stepped into the crack in the cliff and disappeared. Before any of us could ask where he went, Feier jumped down from Jael's shoulder and walked into the cleft, too. Jael followed him, of course, and so did the rest of us.

Once inside, we could see a beam of light coming down from a crack above us. It was much brighter than we expected, and I saw Jon shading his eyes, as he often did in bright light.

"Come here, my children," came Eli's voice. Then he began to sing:

We followed the sound and found ourselves on the edge of a pool. The water in the pool was red, and yet also transparent. I could see the outline of the rock forming the basin it sat in. Eli was standing on the other side of the pool, smiling down at us.

"Here you are at last. Now, no one will make you pay for what is freely given. You may wash and drink of the Living Water to your soul's content. 'Whoever drinks of this water will never thirst'."

We just stood for a few seconds in stunned silence. Then Feier once again broke the spell by padding slowly into the pool. Ripples flowed back from where his little body parted the water. Jael and I slipped in behind him.

The water was cool and refreshing, yet also warm and comfortable. The chill of the night disappeared from my skin immediately, and the weariness of the journey seemed to float off me.

The pool appeared to be shallow when we stood beside it, but once we stepped in, the water was just deep enough to reach to our shoulders, so we could stand or float in it comfortably. I found myself paddling slowly on my back, feeling the wonderful buoyancy as I drifted. It was like being held in someone's arms, like a baby being cuddled and rocked to sleep. I'd never felt so safe and loved in my entire life. When I closed my eyes, time seemed to cease.

Then a sound of splashing water brought me back, and my eyes snapped open. I was next to a small waterfall sending diamond sparkles into the pool and flowing right out of the rock looming above me.

" *'Come, all you who are thirsty, come to the waters; and you who have no money, come, buy and eat! Come and buy wine and milk without money and without cost'.* " I heard Eli's voice chanting rhythmically.

Now I could see the others standing with me beside the little freshet of water. When I put my hands into it, the water felt icy and refreshing. I put my cupped hands to my mouth and drank. I'd never tasted anything so fresh and sweet. I went back for more and kept on drinking until I was fully satisfied.

At long last, I could feel all the dirt washing out of me. My guilt was gone, as though the Lord had taken all of it and rolled it away from me, like a wave on a beach that breaks and then disappears.

Then lights and colors seemed to swirl around me. Red flowed into golds and browns. 'It reminds me of the lamp Jon set on the coffee table in our living room,' came a voice in my head. 'Yes, Ginna,' I thought, 'It does. We may be crossing the GAP.'

CHAPTER 20

THERE IS A RIVER

We were certainly in a new place or time now. My eyes were seeing things that no Earth-bound eyes ever saw, so amazing and glorious it took my breath away. Where looming barren rock had stood, I now saw the towers of a wonderful city with foundations of glowing precious stones, like purple amethyst, red carnelian, golden tiger's eye, green emeralds, and blue sapphires. Doorways opened onto golden shining streets. The lentils around the door-ways were translucent like freshwater pearls, in shades of pink, chocolate, and cream.

"Welcome to the Holy City," came Eli's voice. "The New Zion, The City of the Great King."

"Is it real?" I heard myself ask. I knew the others were near me, but we seemed to be part of a great multitude, streaming through the gates and walking up to the very peak of the city. The streets wound around and climbed steadily, past the most magnificent buildings I'd ever seen. They made The Temple of the Way, back in Tornatoh, look like a pile of old bricks.

As we walked deeper into the city, we came to a sparkling river, which flowed right down the center of the main avenue. Both sides of it were lined with huge, flowering trees.

"This is the River of Life that makes glad the City of God," said Eli. "The fruit of the trees is for the healing of the nations. No one ever hungers or thirsts here. Try some."

We stopped and picked some of the fruit that drooped down right where we could reach it. He was right. It was the most delicious and satisfying thing I ever ate. And a sip of the water from the river was the perfect way to finish off. It had a sweet, tingly flavor, almost like wine or cider. I wondered if the water of the Fountain in the Desert came from the same source.

I could feel myself getting lighter of heart after we ate and drank, as though I'd never be sad again. "There are no more tears, no more sadness here," Eli was saying just then. "The Lord has wiped away all tears from their eyes."

As we neared the top of the city, a vista opened out on a vast paved area shimmering like a huge diamond. At the far end was a great white throne, and seated there was someone so shining and bright I could hardly look at him. Beside him stood a gorgeous woman in a shining white dress.

"Behold the Lamb," voices were singing, "And behold his Bride, the Church."

The air around us was filled with the sounds of the most beautiful music. There were instruments of all kinds, blending in perfect harmony, and voices joining in, each more beautiful than the last. I felt my own lips moving as though I knew the words to the song myself. They just poured out of me of their own accord.

"Is that the King?" I heard Soren ask.

"Yes," said Eli. "He's the Son of God, the Lord of the Universe. In parts of The Book, he's called 'the Lamb of God, who takes away the sin of the world'."

"Is that why we sing 'Behold the Lamb'?" asked Jael.

"We do," Eli nodded. "He's also the 'Lion of Judah', for he was born of this tribe into the world. Most of all he is Kristos, Messiah, the anointed one, the True Lord."

The Bride turned toward us then, and I could see the most blissful smile on her face. It was truly the happiest day of her life. Then the Lord on the throne stood and took her hand, raising it into the air. The multitude around me let out a cheer which sounded like mighty waves crashing on the ocean shore. Even as I watched the newly married pair, they seemed to rise up into a shining cloud.

I was filled with the most unspeakable joy of my life.

***

Suddenly, it was as though a door closed in front of me. The lights and colors were gone. I was standing alone beside the red pool in the cleft of the rock. Tears began to fall from my eyes into the water below me. Then I felt a hand take mine and hold it gently.

"Martina?" came a voice from far away.

"Jon, is that you?"

"Yes. We're back."

"Where did we go?"

"You saw a glimpse of the Lord's Heaven," said Eli.

"How?"

"I helped Jon cross the GAP," he said. "Not all are permitted this vision."

"It was too wonderful for words," I sighed. "I know I'll never see anything like it again."

"Until we go to be with the Lord," Eli whispered.

Jon pulled himself closer to me, and put his arm across my shoulders. I found myself settling back into his embrace, feeling so natural there.

"The Bride was so beautiful, and so happy," I sighed.

"Yes, she was the personification of all who believe in the Lord," Eli said.

"Jael, are you here?" I asked suddenly.

"Right here with Feier."

"Where's Soren?" Jon asked.

We all looked around and realized we didn't see him.

"It was his time to stay," said Eli quietly.

"You mean he stayed there?" Jael murmured.

"Yes," said Eli. "He's in Heaven."

"So we know he's happy," I said. "But I'll miss him. I was just getting to know him."

"Me too," said Jon. "I feel blessed to have spent the time with him I did. You know, now that I've seen Heaven, I know in my heart *it* is our true home. I wish I could've stayed there, too. All my life I've been searching—and leaving places I thought were home. But now I see home is ahead of me, and I'm still on the journey. But what a wonderful home it will be."

His voice broke off, and I could see tears in his eyes.

"You know, I think I finally understand how hugely the Lord loves us," I said.

"Me, too," said Jon.

"To think he left such a wonderful and amazing place to come here."

"And not only that, but to die for us." Jael said.

"In spite of all the bad things we humans have done," added Jon.

"That has to be the most amazing love ever," I sighed.

"But I love *you*, Martina."

I took Jon's hand. "Your love is amazing, too—to think you love me in spite of all I've done."

"As The Book says, 'We love because he first loved us'," said Eli.

Jon was looking at me intently. "Martina, I've never seen you look so beautiful. You're actually glowing."

I turned to look into his eyes. "You are, too," I whispered.

"You've been in the Lord's presence," Eli said. "Now that your guilt is washed away, you can reflect his glory for all your world to see."

We just stood there awhile, hand-in-hand, gazing into each other's eyes.

"Eli?" I murmured, barely able to get my voice to work. "Jon and I need to be married before the Lord of Heaven. I finally see that now."

He smiled. "You can make your promises and vows right here."

Jon put his arm around my waist and pulled me closer. "Yes, at the Fountain."

Eli took our hands and pressed them together with his own. "Do you, Jon, take Martina to be your wife—to care for her in all things—until you part in death?"

"Yes," whispered Jon.

"And Martina, do you take Jon to be your husband—to care for him in all things—until you part in death?"

"Yes, I do."

The old man gently squeezed our hands together and then let go. "You may kiss your wife," he said softly. "You're now officially married, in the Lord's eyes, as well as the world's."

Jon gathered me into his arms and gave me the most wonderful kiss I ever had.

With this settled, my next thoughts were of our baby. "Jon, how fast can we get back to Celeton?"

"In the blink of an eye, since I have the coordinates."

"That would be wonderful. I miss Celestia so much."

His arm tightened around my shoulders. "Me, too," he sighed. "Jael, are you ready?"

"Sure." He picked up Feier in his arms. "Are you coming, Eli?"

"No, young one. I have other pilgrims to meet."

Jon shook the old man's hand then. "Thank you so much, Eli. We couldn't have found the Fountain without you."

"This is my calling," he smiled.

Then his face began to blur and shimmer. I could almost feel Jon closing his eyes, and pulling me and Jael closer to him, as we entered the GAP.

CHAPTER 21

REUNION

As soon as we came out of the GAP, I saw Donmal looking at us with expectant eyes. I dreaded, in a way, telling him that his friend Soren wasn't with us, but I knew I should be the one to tell him. I'd come to enjoy Soren's company during our travels, and knew him as well as any of us.

So I took his hand first. "Donmal, I wanted to be the one to tell you Soren is in Heaven."

I was surprised when he just nodded and gave a half smile. "He told me he was thinking it was his time." Then he pulled me toward a bed I hadn't seen before.

"Father?" My voice spoke before my brain even registered.

The figure on the bed smiled and sighed, "I knew you would think that. No, I'm his twin, Dominic, your uncle."

"Uncle Dominic!" Then it all fell into place, and I turned to Donmal. "He's *your* father!"

"Yes, Martina. Did you forget Darien told you we're cousins?"

I was ashamed to admit I did forget for a moment. The shock of seeing someone who looked so much like Father turned my brain to mush. But Donmal wasn't finished yet.

"There's someone else who came with him who'd really like to see you, Martina."

In that instant, I saw the woman with long dark hair like mine step into the room. Before I could even react, Jael threw himself toward her. But she had to step back because she was holding a baby—my Celestia.

"Mother!" Jael cried.

I was still numb. Slowly, I walked toward her, whispering, "Is it really you, Mother?"

"Of course it is, my sweet daughter. And how wonderful to have a granddaughter."

Then we both lost it and collapsed into each other's arms, baby and all. Jael was dancing around us, as we stood there together and wept.

Finally, we managed to disengage, and I stepped back. "How did you get here, Mother? We thought you were lost in the Terres-City disaster."

"I nearly was," she said. "I wouldn't be here if it weren't for people the Lord sent to help me—like Dominic, and his friend Jakob—you will meet him, and Myra, soon. But the one who deserves the most credit, for she found me sitting in a fountain and helped me out of the City—a young girl who never gave up."

Now I could see a girl stepping out of the shadows, with red hair and cheeks flushed pink. She was about Jael's height, and I recognized the shape of her face, like Jason's.

"Irina," she said, "You deserve a lot of credit for getting *me* here, and you know it."

Jael turned at her voice and dashed straight into her arms, "Raina!" he cried. "You did survive! Somehow I knew you weren't dead."

"I knew you were alive, too, Jael. I'm so glad your God kept me alive to see you again."

"You should've seen what we just saw in his Heaven." Jael said then. "It was the most awesome, amazing—"

"Words can't really express it," I said.

"I'd like to hear about it, too," said a soft feminine voice.

Jael turned to look, and both he and Jon exclaimed together, "Daiah! How did *you* get here?"

"Dominic, my friend, helped me," she smiled.

We all stood looking at each other in awe, the ones seemingly back from the 'dead', and the ones just returned from the Fountain in the Desert.

"All of us have a lot of sharing to do," said Jon.

"That's for sure," said Darien.

CHAPTER 22

BLIND NO LONGER

[*"Martina."*

"Yes, Ginna?"

"Does this mean I have to go back now?"

"I think so."

"I really don't want to go back."

"Well, that's interesting. I seem to remember when we started this journey, you were worried about not being able to get back."

"But now I want to stay here and keep being you. Your wedding was so beautiful."

"You'll have a wedding of your own someday."

"I wonder if I'll ever get married."

"Just wait. The Lord has big plans for you in your own life."

"But I like your life better than mine."

"Now, Ginna," came Jon's voice. "You need to live your own life, you know."

"And Danny needs to live his, too," added Jael.

"That's right, Sis," Danny said. "I can't go back without you. You're an important part of my life."

"But why?" Ginna's eyes were filling with tears. "I need someone like Jon to take care of me, like you have, Martina."

Martina took both Ginna's hands in hers. "I know it's frightening sometimes, Ginna. I've been right where you are. You've seen it with me in the GAP. Your life is ahead of you, though. It's an empty page ready to be written on, and it's much better if we each write our own story with the Lord's help."

Jon stepped closer and took one of her hands. "Right now, our lives look more exciting than yours, but really there's not much difference. So we traveled to other planets, but you'll also go to many places in your life. Your experiences will be just as rich in their own time, believe me."

"Okay," she sighed deeply. "But promise you'll still come when I call?"

"Remember a call comes of itself. You can't decide to call us," said Jael.

"I know."]

The air began to swirl around her, colors fading to brown, and all she could feel was Jon's hand in hers. Then it was as though his hand dissolved into the air. She reached out desperately for something to grab and found another smaller hand.

"I'm here, Sis," came Danny's voice.

Gradually the swirling stopped, and her eyes made out the familiar shapes of their living room, the old couch with the same sag and stains on the upholstery, and the coffee table with the same old scratches.

"I guess we're back—all alone," she muttered.

"Not quite," Danny said. "We still have each other."

This made her stop suddenly and look at her brother, realizing she'd been taking him for granted recently.

"Danny, I'm sorry I've been so hard on you the past couple of years."

He reached for her, and patted her shoulder gently. "Hey, it's all right, Sis."

"No, it's really not. Being 'in' Martina, I noticed how when she was upset or worried about something, she took it out on Jon or Jael. That's what I've been doing to you, letting my anger lash out for the wrong reasons. Will you please forgive me?"

"Of course I will, Ginna. After all, we're still a family. We have Mom, even though Dad left."

"That still hurts, you know."

"That's why we need to be here for each other, and not get angry over something that's not our fault."

She pulled him into a big hug. "Thanks, Little Brother."

Danny smiled, remembering how Jon called Jael this. Then he pointed toward the couch. "Look what Jon gave us."

Ginna opened her eyes wider and realized there was a little brown-striped kitten sitting in the middle of the couch cushion.

"Is that Feier?" she asked in disbelief.

"Not quite," said Danny. "He's an earth-cat, not a feier-cat. But Jon gave him to us, to help us remember our journeys within Martina and Jael."

"As if we could ever forget them."

Moving very gently, he picked up the kitten, who started to purr. When he handed it to his sister, she pulled it close to her cheek, and rubbed the kitten's face.

"I love you, kitten," she whispered. "What shall we call you?"

"Jon said it's a boy," whispered Danny. "I was thinking Jael."

"No." She shook her head. "I think we should call him Soren."

"You know, that does sound like a good name."

"It will remind us of what we saw of Heaven. We're on the same journey toward home, too. And maybe we'll see the real Soren there someday."

PREVIEW OF
THE PEAKS SAGA, BOOK 4

"WHEN THE WORLD GROWS COLD"

CHAPTER 1

AMID THE SNOW

Annemarie Parker leaned out the open hotel window, watching a world of softly drifting flakes, while the wind teased her long blonde hair. For an instant, she could visualize herself out there, floating slowly with those flakes, drifting ever downward, coming at last to rest in a wet spot on the sidewalk below.

'Just to rest. That's what I need,' she thought.

But her only movement was to hold out her hand and watch as the white fluffy flakes landed there, began to sag and settle, and finally disappeared, in tiny wet drops that slipped through her fingers. Just like her thoughts—sagging, melting, and disappearing into a dark chill night.

Her eyes tried to focus through the swirling whiteness. Out there loomed the indistinct shapes of downtown Denver, buildings that should be looking back at her with lighted windows for eyes, but this night they were blurred shapes, with their lights diffused by the snow in the air. Now her eyes began to blur, but not from the snow. These drops were warm, and fell onto her cheeks.

'There are too many memories here,' she sighed to herself. 'I should never have come back.'

Her ears could almost hear the strumming of guitars—hers and David's—and the singing of their Gospel group, along with the laughter of friends long-gone from her life. 'Yes, we used to sing here a lot, in this very hotel—there was a youth gathering right after Christmas every year.'

The words of the songs had meant so much then: 'The Old Rugged Cross' and 'Love Lifted Me'.

And there was always lots of snow, which made it all the more cozy. The memories seemed to shine like Christmas, as she saw them now in her mind. So many times she'd sat at a window, just like this, watching the snow turn the world into a dream—a place of beauty and love.

But she'd been much younger then—what was it? Nearly eight years ago? Life hadn't seemed so confusing at that time—everything had been more simple and natural, like the first time David held her hand.

He'd been walking her home from church—back in their little hometown of Deer Path, Colorado. They sang almost every Sunday when they were in high school. Gradually other members of their Gospel group moved on to college or jobs, until she and David were the only ones left.

Her mother, Ginna Parker, usually drove home before Annemarie was ready to leave. Mom didn't stay to visit much after church. Most of the time, David had a new song he wanted her to learn, and they'd practice for almost an hour before heading home. But Deer Path was so small, anyone could walk from one end to the other in an hour or less.

Sometimes Uncle Danny hung around to listen to them practice. He seemed to really enjoy their music. Annemarie knew her mother could take it or leave it. But Ginna's life hadn't been easy, she knew. After all, when a local girl got pregnant and decided to keep the baby, that was big news in such a small town. Besides, Ginna and her brother Danny were always considered outsiders, not having spent their whole lives in Deer Path. Annemarie had—at least through high school.

But she seemed to have a restless nature. She never met her father, or even knew his name. No one seemed to be able to tell her anything about him. Ginna refused to say anything—ever—about this mystery man. So, Annemarie lived with the whispers. Was he a drifter who was just passing through? Perhaps someone else in the town? Only Ginna knew, and she'd apparently worn herself to silence.

Growing up with all the talk behind her back—and even to her face—Annemarie knew she must be very careful. Her mother seemed to sigh with relief when she began spending time with David. He was the pastor's son, and apparently wanted to live up to his father's expectations. It wasn't surprising, then, that they walked across the small town many Sundays before he finally took her hand.

Now she tried to remember the thrill of that first touch. It had been such a strong feeling then—a warmth coursing all through her body. Their hands seemed to fit together perfectly, as though they were made for each other. And later, there was the first kiss.

But all these memories were getting blurred now—as hazy and fuzzy as the snow-filled world outside her window. A large tear plopped on the windowsill, and her heart ached with the questions she couldn't answer.

'What happened? Which of us changed? How could something seeming so right go so wrong? Perhaps I've inherited a curse from my mother,' she said to herself. She didn't want to blame Ginna, but sometimes she couldn't help it. 'Her choices—bad or not—have caused me a lot of pain,' she muttered. But then she sighed, for she knew if she was honest, most of her pain was caused by her own choices—and there was really no one else to blame but herself.

She stood and shivered, reaching toward the top of the window. Just as she was trying to get up the courage to climb onto the sill, she saw a shape out there in the snow-filled air. It seemed to be a face, but the eyes were like stars shining, and the long hair was billowing out into the cold air, like sails on a great ship. She gasped in fear and froze, unable to close the window or to drop her hand from the sash.

Then a gust of wind rushed past her face. She could see swirls of white as snow whirled into the room. Stepping back, she covered her face with her hands, trying not to scream. When she slowly pulled her hands down and tried to focus her eyes, there was a young woman with long dark hair standing in the room with her.

A long-ago conversation with her mother came into her mind, and she remembered a name: "Martina?" she said. "Mom mentioned someone named Martina once, but I don't remember anything else, except that she had long, dark hair—and she took her somewhere."

"Well, I'm her daughter, Celestia. Did she tell you anything about me?"

Annemarie glanced down at the floor and tried to think, but her mind was just a whirl. A few minutes ago she'd been contemplating suicide, and now here she was talking to this stranger who appeared out of the sky. 'Am I hallucinating?' she wondered.

Finally, she found her voice, "No, I don't remember anything else. Mom was always very close-mouthed about her past. She never told me anything about my father."

"Okay," Celestia sighed. "Well, to start with, I'm a GAP-Crosser—or what some might call a time-traveler. Jon, my father, is the one who's done the most exploration of the Time-GAP's possibilities, and he taught me some of what he knows. At first, GAP-crossing was used mainly to travel great distances through the Galaxy. Only first-born have the power to learn to manipulate the GAP, which stands for Galactic Antipaterminal Passage, by the way. This dimension of space/time has always existed, but here in your time people haven't yet discovered this potential of the first-born. I guess right now, you might call it a sort of 'worm hole'."

"I've heard that term in science videos," Annemarie nodded. "But what does all this have to do with me? And how did you get here?"

"I crossed the GAP," she smiled. "My father and my Uncle Jael have learned how to cross Time-GAPs."

"You mean like a Time Portal?"

"Yeah, I think that's what they called it back in this century."

"So you're from the future?" It was difficult to keep the disbelief out of her voice.

Celestia just smiled and nodded to her. "I can't explain all the technical stuff. All I know is what Dad taught me. About twenty-five years ago, in Earth years, he and Jael came to your mother and your Uncle Danny."

"Here to Colorado?"

"Yes, to their little town of Deer Path."

"That's where I grew up—and I'm twenty-five years old now."

"I know." Again, Celestia smiled, and this time there seemed to be some secret knowledge in her expression. "Anyway, they took your mom, Ginna, and her brother to their time—into the distant future, to share their stories with them. Actually, they crossed the GAP more than once. The last time, Dad did an experiment that had something to do with parallel universes."

"Now wait a minute—this is starting to sound like science fiction." Annemarie shook her head in disbelief. "Are you just making this up as you go along?"

Celestia patted her arm. "No, I'm trying to tell you the truth. It appears you've called me, like your mother did mine."

In her conscious mind, Annemarie wanted to pull away from Celestia's touch, but something in her subconscious held her back. The longer she felt that gentle touch, the calmer she began to feel. "Okay," she sighed, "I'll suspend my disbelief—for now."

"I'm glad, because this gets even stranger." Again, Celestia had a knowing smile in her eyes. "What Jon, my father, did was merge Danny with Jael, and Ginna with Martina, my mother. They became like two minds in one body."

"They what? Okay, I'm really having trouble with this."

"I know, Annemarie." Again, the woman's touch seemed to be saying even more than her voice. "It's really difficult to explain. But while your mother was 'within' *my* mother, Martina, she experienced everything with her. They were both 'there', in a sense. Did your mom ever tell you anything about this?"

Annemarie shook her head, but then stopped as an image came into her mind. "All she ever said was the name Martina once, and a strange journey they'd taken together. But there was one other time, when I was about fourteen years old. We were sitting on a new living-room couch we'd just bought. Suddenly her eyes seemed to get a faraway look in them and I heard her whisper, 'I wonder if it was something in the old couch that made it possible.' I asked her what she meant, but she suddenly shook her head, and seemed not to remember even saying anything. Then she looked out the window and added, 'I think it was all a dream'."

"Dad says many people think of it as a dream. But I'm here to prove to you, and maybe your mother, that it really did happen."

"So what happens now? Do you take *me* to some other place or time?"

"Actually, this time is different. First you get to tell me your story."

"You don't really want to hear my story," she muttered. "It's not a pretty one."

"Well, the ones my parents came to share with your mother and uncle weren't exactly pretty, either. But they were true, and they all taught each of them some truth about life, and the Lord of the Universe."

"You mean God?"

"Yes, some people call him that."

"Do you think my story can teach *you* something?"

Celestia shrugged. "Perhaps. And someday, I may be able to share mine with you. I think we can both learn something from each other. But my directions said you were to start first."

"Your directions? Who gave those?"

"I can't explain in a way you'll understand right now. Maybe later."

"Okay. This means I have to start, I guess."

"In a minute. First I need to get this lamp lit."

Celestia produced an amber-colored lamp with a strange fluted chimney—Annemarie had no idea where it came from. She set it on the bedside table, because there wasn't another level spot in the small hotel room. Annemarie didn't see how she lit it, but soon swirls of gold, amber, and brown were slowly moving around the walls of the room.

The two young women sat down on the bed at the same time. This brought shy smiles to both their faces.

Then Celestia reached over and took Annemarie's hands in hers, and again there seemed to be a warm calm flowing into her from the time-traveler's touch.

"You may start anytime you feel ready," she said. "I'm firstborn and can cross the GAP. And the Lantern will take us wherever we may need to go, especially in the fourth dimension—Time."

Thank you!

Thank you for joining me. If you liked the story and have a minute to spare, I would appreciate a short comment on the page or site where you bought the book.

Reviews from readers like you make a huge difference to helping new readers find stories similar to The Peaks series: *Mountaintops and Valleys.*

- Amazon
- Barnes & Noble
- Goodreads
- iBooks

Thank you!

M. F. Erler

ABOUT THE AUTHOR

M.F. Erler has been writing since she was about 14 years old. In fact, some of the initial ideas and characters for "The Peaks at the Edge of the World" were conceived when she was in high school, while writing assignments for freshman English class. Her lifelong goal has been to get the Peaks Trilogy out to readers, and thanks to new developments in electronic publishing, her dream has been fulfilled.

Fantasy and Science Fiction have long been among her favorite reading materials, and her favorite authors are C.S. Lewis and J.R.R. Tolkien. She is also interested in history, comparative religion, ecology, and music. Her previous publications include non-fiction articles in "Today's Christian Parent" and "Social Studies and the Young Learner." She has worked as an Environmental

Education teacher and facilitator, and also as a music teacher. Hobbies include reading, playing several musical instruments, and needlework.

She and her husband, Paul, have two adult children. All make their home in the Pacific Northwest.

Contact Frances at mferler@peaksandbeyond.com
Or follow her blog at PeaksAndBeyond.com